HUCKLEBERRY
Finished

Books by Livia J. Washburn

FRANKLY MY DEAR, I'M DEAD

HUCKLEBERRY FINISHED

Published by Kensington Publishing Corporation

HUCKLEBERRY
Finished

LIVIA J. WASHBURN

KENSINGTON BOOKS
http://www.kensingtonbooks.com

KENSINGTON BOOKS are published by

Kensington Publishing Corp.
119 West 40th Street
New York, New York 10018

ISBN-13: 978-0-7582-2567-2
ISBN-10: 0-7582-2567-9

First Hardcover Printing: November 2009
First Mass Market Printing: November 2010
10 9 8 7 6 5 4 3 2 1

Printed in the United States of America

For Larry and Karen Mackey,
with thanks for their help
on rebuilding our home.

CHAPTER 1

Mark Twain once wrote, "I can picture that old time to myself now, just as it was then . . . the great Mississippi, the majestic, the magnificent Mississippi, rolling its mile-wide tide along, shining in the sun."

As I stood at the railing of the *Southern Belle*, I knew what he meant. I had seldom seen anything quite so beautiful and serene as the great river. Sure, the scenery along the banks wasn't as pristine and unspoiled as it was back in Twain's day. I could see tall fast-food signs and electrical lines and jets winging across the blue summer sky. But out here in the middle of the river all I could hear were the gentle rumble of the boat's engines and the splashing of the paddlewheels as they propelled us through the water at a sedate pace. I felt the faint vibrations of the engine through the deck, and the sun was warm on my face. If you closed your eyes, I thought, it would almost seem like you were really back there and Sam Clemens himself was up in the pilothouse, guiding the riverboat toward the next quaint little river town where it would dock.

And then somebody's dadgum cell phone rang.

"Yellll-o!"

That's the way he said it, swear to God.

"Yeah, guess where we are? . . . We're on a riverboat! . . . Yeah, on the Mississippi. Helen wanted to come. But it's so freakin' slow, I think I could walk faster! Haw, haw!"

My hands tightened on the smooth, polished wood of the railing. I figured I'd better hold on, because a good travel agent never punches her clients. That's one of the first rules they teach you.

"What? . . . No, damn it, I told him those reports had to be finished by yesterday . . . What's he been doing this whole time, sitting around with his thumb up his—"

I couldn't let him go on. I turned around and said, "Sir!"

He looked surprised at the interruption. He was a big guy, balding, with the beginnings of a beer gut in a polo shirt. Played college football, from the looks of him, but that was more than twenty years in the past. Beside him, wearing a visor, sunglasses, a sleeveless blue blouse, and baggy white shorts, was a blond woman carrying a big straw purse and a long-suffering look. She was married to the loudmouth, more than likely.

He said, "Hold on, Larry," into the cell phone,

then took it away from his ear. "Yeah? What can I do for you?"

About a dozen other members of my tour group had lined up along the railing. I gestured vaguely toward them and said, "These folks are tryin' to, you know, soak up the ambience of the river, and your business conversation is a little jarring."

"I'm sorry"—he didn't sound like he meant it—"but I got a crisis on my hands here."

"I understand that. Maybe you could go inside to talk to your associate."

He shook his head. "My crappy phone won't work in there. I'm barely getting any reception out here." He put the crappy phone back to his ear and went on, "Larry, you still there? You tell that worthless little weasel to get those reports done by the end of the day or he's fired! You got that? And if any of this comes back on *my* head, he ain't gonna be the only one, *capeesh*?"

I didn't know whether to be mad at him for ignoring me or flabbergasted at the guy's language. I couldn't remember the last time I'd heard anybody say "Capeesh?"

"Yeah, yeah, you and Holloway both know where you can put your excuses. Just take care of it."

He snapped the phone closed, looked at me, raised his eyebrows, and shrugged his shoulders as if to say, *Now are you satisfied, lady?*

I managed to say, "Thank you."

He rolled his eyes, shook his head, and moved off down the railing toward the stern.

His wife lingered long enough to say, "I'm

sorry, Ms. Dickinson. Eddie's just very devoted to his business."

"That's all right, Mrs. Kramer," I told her. I had finally remembered their names. "I understand."

I didn't, not really, but that's what you tell people anyway. I didn't understand why people would pay good money to take a vacation and then bring their work with them. I was devoted to my business, too, but if I were getting away from it, I'd get as far away as I could and stay there until it was time to go home.

Louise Kramer smiled at me and then followed her husband along the deck. He had already opened his phone and was talking on it again, but at least he wasn't disturbing the other members of the group as much.

The *Southern Belle* had started upriver from St. Louis about an hour earlier, after the forty members of my tour group had gotten together for lunch at a restaurant not far from the riverfront. I had booked a private room so that we could eat together, and then everyone had gotten up and introduced himself or herself. I don't think that everybody who goes on one of my tours has to be all buddy-buddy with the other clients, but since we were all going to be together on a relatively small boat for the next twenty-four hours I didn't think it would hurt for them to get to know each other. After all, some people go on vacation tours *hoping* that they'll meet someone who'll turn out to be special in their lives.

Most folks, though, just want the scenery and

the history. And, in the case of the *Southern Belle*, the gambling. The side-wheeler was a floating casino.

Casino gambling is legal in most places up and down the Mississippi River, and there are numerous riverboats devoted to that purpose. Most of them are permanently docked, however. Some even have the engines gutted out so that they'll never move again, at least not under their own power.

The *Southern Belle* was a little different. Built in the late nineteenth century, it had been lovingly restored and refurbished under the supervision of its current owner, a real estate mogul named Charles Gallister. From what I'd heard, he owned half the shopping centers in the greater St. Louis area.

In addition to being a very successful businessman, he was a Mark Twain buff. Because of his interest in the man some consider to be the greatest American author, Gallister had bought the riverboat and set up these overnight cruises to Hannibal, Missouri, the town where young Sam Clemens had grown up.

Gallister had the golden touch in more than real estate, too. Rumor had it that he was making a small fortune from the gambling that took place on the *Southern Belle*.

All I knew for sure was that it was a powerful draw. When I decided to add the riverboat cruise to the list of literary-oriented tours that my little agency in Atlanta books, I hadn't had any trouble filling it up. This was the first time my clients had gone on the tour, so I figured I'd better come along, too, just to make sure there were no glitches. I had flown to St. Louis, leaving my daughter and son-in-law back in Atlanta to hold down the fort at the office.

I had been running tours like this for nearly a year. Thanks to a suggestion from a friend of mine, an English professor named Will Burke, I had concentrated on tours with some sort of literary angle. The *Gone With the Wind* tour, which included an overnight stay at a working plantation designed to resemble Tara from the book and the movie, was the most popular. Which sort of surprised me considering the fact that there had been a couple of murders on the plantation the very first time I ran the tour.

Since then I'd been a little leery of trouble every time I added a new tour to my list, but so far everything had gone smoothly. I didn't have any reason to expect that this riverboat cruise would be any different.

Laughter from the tourists attracted my attention. I turned to see a man in a rumpled white suit ambling along the deck. He had a shock of white hair, a bushy white mustache, and carried an unlit cigar in his hand. He nodded to the tourists and said, "It could probably be shown by facts and figures that there is no distinctly native American criminal class . . . except Congress."

That brought more laughter and applause. The white-suited man waved his cigar in acknowledgment and went on, "I'll be dispensing more of the wit and wisdom of the immortal

Mark Twain tonight in the salon, at eight o'clock. Thank you."

The tourists applauded again. The Twain impersonator continued along the deck, coming toward me. He stayed in character for the most part, stooping over, shuffling his feet, and walking like an old man.

He greeted me with a nod and said in his gruff Twain voice, "Good afternoon, young lady."

"Hello, Mr. Twain," I said. I held out my hand to him. "I'm Delilah Dickinson. I put together one of the tour groups on the boat."

He took my hand. His hand was a giveaway that he wasn't as old as the character he was playing. His grip was that of a much younger man.

"Very pleased to meet you, Ms. Dickinson. I quite fancy redheaded women, you know. I'm Samuel Langhorne Clemens."

"You know, I can almost believe that," I told him with a smile. "You've got the look and the voice down."

He waved the cigar. "Thank you, thank you." He leaned closer and half whispered, "You can't tell that I'm new at the job?"

That took me by surprise. He looked and sounded like he'd been playing Mark Twain for a long time.

"Not at all," I told him. "You must be a quick study."

He shrugged. "I have some acting experience." His real voice was also that of a younger man. "My name actually is Mark . . . Mark Lansing."

"I'm pleased to meet Mr. Lansing as well as Mr. Twain."

I was happy that he'd referred to me as a young lady, too. When you get to be my age, which I refer to as the late mumbly-mumblies, and you're divorced and have a grown, married daughter, you don't often feel all that young. I was just vain enough to enjoy the attention from Mark Lansing, even though in reality he might be younger than me.

"Will you be attending my performance tonight?" he asked.

"I hadn't really thought about it—"

"I'd appreciate it if you would. I could use a friendly face in the audience. Like I said, I'm new at this."

"Well, all right, sure. I'll be there," I promised.

"I hope you won't be disappointed." He lifted a hand in farewell. "I have to circulate among the other decks and the casino. See you later."

He shuffled off—not to Buffalo—and I went over to the members of my tour group who had gathered along the rail to ask them if anybody had any questions or needed any help with anything. Nobody did.

That gave me a chance to go back to my cabin for a few minutes and call the office. Unlike Eddie Kramer's cell phone, mine worked just fine inside the boat.

Luke Edwards, my son-in-law, answered. "Dickinson Literary Tours."

"Hey, Luke, it's me."

"Miz D! Are you on the riverboat?"

"I sure am. Everything's going just fine, too. I met Mark Twain a few minutes ago."

"Really? The guy who wrote *Huckleberry Finn?*" Luke hesitated. "Wait a minute. He's dead. He can't be on that riverboat."

"No, but an actor playing him is."

"Oh. That makes sense, I guess."

"Is Melissa there?" Luke is big and handsome and charming as all get-out with the clients, but Melissa has a lot better head for business.

"No, she's gone to the office supply place to pick up some stuff."

"Any problems since I've been gone?"

"Uh, Miz D, you only left this morning. We've been able to manage just fine for the past five hours."

"I know, I know. Anybody else sign up for that New Orleans tour yet?"

"Nope. Of course, I haven't checked the Web site in the past five minutes. Somebody could've e-mailed us about it."

"Why don't you do that?"

"Right now? Really?"

I sighed. "No, you're right. I need to just relax and enjoy this tour I'm on. What's the point in being a travel agent if you can't get some fun out of it yourself?"

"That's it exactly. Just relax and let us take care of everything here. It'll be fine. You'll see."

"All right. Tell Melissa I called, okay?"

"Will do. Don't worry about a thing."

"I won't. Love ya both."

"Love you, too," he told me. I knew he meant it. They were good kids, both of them.

I closed my cell phone and slipped it back in the pocket of my blazer. Real estate agents and tour guide leaders would be lost without blazers. And everything was going along so smoothly that I was sort of at a loss to know what to do next.

I know, I know. I couldn't have jinxed myself any worse than by thinking such a thing. That realization occurred to me just as somebody knocked on the door of my cabin.

CHAPTER 2

I was muttering something to myself about being nine different kinds of darned fool when I opened the door and saw one of the riverboat's stewards standing just outside my cabin, which opened onto the deck.

"Ms. Dickinson, ma'am?"

"That's right."

"There's a, uh, problem with one of the members of your tour group in the casino's main room. Could you come with me?"

"Sure," I said. "Lead the way." As we hurried along the deck I asked, "What sort of trouble?" I had visions of somebody winning a jackpot and having a heart attack, or something like that.

"I couldn't really say, ma'am. Mr. Rafferty just asked me to see if I could find you. One of the members of your group told me you'd gone to your cabin."

He wasn't claiming not to know what the trouble was; he just wasn't allowed to tell me. That's what it sounded like, anyway.

"Who's this fella Rafferty?"

"Mr. Rafferty's the head of security for the *Southern Belle*."

Uh-oh. There went the hope that this was something minor and easily brushed aside. The head of security didn't get involved unless the problem was an important one.

We came to a set of fancy double doors with lots of gleaming wood, gilt curlicues, and stained glass. They opened into a foyer with parquet flooring and several windows where pretty girls sat at cash registers. Gamblers bought chips there for the various games and cashed them in when they were done. If they were lucky enough to have any winnings, that is. The unlucky ones just came back and bought more chips.

On the other side of the foyer was the casino's main room. It looked just like what you'd see in a Vegas casino, only on a smaller scale. A couple dozen slot machines instead of hundreds. Poker tables, roulette wheels, faro layouts. Garish lighting. Music blaring from concealed speakers. Laughter, smoke, the *chunk-chunk-chunk* of slot machine wheels turning over, the clicking of the little white ball dancing merrily around the roulette wheel, the occasional whoop of triumph or groan of despair . . . It was a seductive atmosphere, all right, but it seemed as far removed from the sedate and stately Mississippi as if it had been on the moon.

The steward nervously touched my arm to guide me across the room. "This way, ma'am."

"Where are we going?"

"The security office, ma'am."

That's what I had figured. Somebody was being detained.

I hoped they weren't about to boot whoever it was off the boat.

The steward took me to a nondescript metal door. The short hallway behind it was strictly functional. It ended at some carpeted stairs that led up to the next deck. At the top of the stairs was a large open area equipped with numerous computers and monitors. A low, almost inaudible hum filled the air. The feeds from all the security cameras on board wound up here, I assumed. None of the men and women sitting at the monitors looked around as the steward took me to another door. He knocked on this one.

"Come in," a man called.

The office on the other side of the door was spacious and comfortably furnished with a big desk, a leather-covered sofa, a plasma TV hanging on the wall, and a window that looked out on the river. Two men waited in the office, one on the sofa, the other behind the desk. Both of them stood up when I came in. The one behind the desk was deliberate about it. The one on the sofa jumped to his feet.

"Ms. Dickinson," the one from the sofa said. "I'm sorry. I didn't mean to cause trouble."

I remembered him from the luncheon in St. Louis earlier that afternoon. "What's happened here, Mr. Webster?" I asked him.

His name was Ben Webster. He was in his mid to late twenties, I'd say, with fairly close-cropped dark hair and what seemed to be a perpetually solemn expression. His age and the fact that he was traveling alone made him a little unusual for one of my clients. I get a lot of families and middle-aged and older couples. Not to over-generalize, but most young men these days aren't that interested in seeing where Mark Twain or Margaret Mitchell or Tennessee Williams lived and worked.

Which meant that Ben Webster was probably here for the gambling, so I wasn't particularly surprised to find him in the casino. I was surprised that he seemed to be in trouble, though. He had seemed like a nice, polite young man in the short time we had talked together at lunch. He even reminded me a little of Luke.

"I'm sorry, but I couldn't let it pass," he said now. "That roulette wheel is rigged. I saw the man working it run his finger over the same little mark on the table several times while it was spinning, and then all the big bets lost. There must be a pressure switch of some sort there, or maybe an optical one built into the table."

The man behind the desk let Webster get his complaint out without saying anything. But he wore a tolerant smile and shook his head slowly while the young man spoke.

When Webster was finished, the man stepped out from behind the desk and extended a big hand toward me. "Ms. Dickinson, I'm Logan Rafferty, the head of security for the *Southern Belle.* I'm sorry we couldn't meet under more pleasant circumstances."

Like his hand, which pretty much swallowed mine whole, the rest of Logan Rafferty was big.

He was about forty, with a brown brush cut, and although he wore an expensive suit, he looked like he'd be just as much at home working as a bouncer in a roadhouse somewhere. The afternoon sunlight that came in through the window winked on a heavy ring he wore.

"What seems to be the trouble here, Mr. Rafferty?"

He inclined his head toward Ben Webster. "As you just heard, a member of your tour group has a complaint about the way the games are run in the casino. I assure you, all our games are conducted in an honest, legitimate manner." A faint smile appeared on his face. "As you may know, the odds always favor the house to start with. We see no need to tilt them even more."

"No offense, but I would think you'd be used to folks complaining when they lose. It's sort of human nature, after all," I said.

"Complaints we don't mind," Rafferty said with a shrug of his big shoulders. "We don't like it when passengers try to slug one of our employees, though."

I frowned at Ben Webster. "You *didn't*?"

He hung his head and didn't say anything.

I turned back to Rafferty. "I'm sorry," I began. "I hope there wasn't too much of a ruckus. I didn't see any signs of trouble while we were coming through the casino."

"No, things got back to normal quickly once the commotion was over," Rafferty admitted. "And there wasn't much commotion to start with. My security personnel were on the scene before Mr. Webster here could do any real damage."

"I'm sorry," I said again. "What do we need to do to put this matter behind us?"

"The man who operates the roulette wheel could press charges, you know."

I wasn't sure what law enforcement agency had jurisdiction over the Mississippi River. There was bound to be one, though. I said, "Do we really have to get the law involved in this? I was hopin' we could sort it out amongst ourselves, you know?"

"Webster gets off the boat in Hannibal and doesn't get back aboard." The words came out of Rafferty's mouth hard and flat, like there was no room for negotiation. That suited him more. He just wasn't the affable type, no matter how hard he tried.

Webster's head came up. "You can't do that," he said. "I paid for a round-trip. And my car's in St. Louis."

"You can rent a car in Hannibal and drive back down to St. Louis," Rafferty said. "As for what you paid, that's between you and Ms. Dickinson. But as far as the *Southern Belle* is concerned, you're not welcome on board." He went behind his desk and leaned forward, resting his knuckles on the glass top. "Or I can make a phone call and have the authorities waiting when we dock in Hannibal to *take* you off the boat."

"I'm sure that won't be necessary," I said. I turned to look at Ben Webster. "Will it?"

I don't know if he saw the pleading in my eyes, but after a second he shrugged and said, "No, it won't be necessary. I'll leave the boat. It's not fair, though. That guy really was cheating."

Rafferty's mouth tightened into a thin line. I thought Webster had pushed him too far. But all he said was, "You can go back to your cabin now, Mr. Webster, and stay there. The casino is off limits to you."

"Fine," Webster muttered. "I don't want to lose any more money to your crooked games anyway."

It was all I could do not to grab him by the collar and shake him. Either that or smack him on the back of the head. Didn't he know he was getting off easy? They send people to jail for attacking other people.

I took hold of his arm and steered him toward the door. "Let's go, Mr. Webster."

Behind us, Rafferty said, "I hope to see you again during the cruise, Ms. Dickinson. Do you need someone to show you out?"

"No, thanks. I remember the way I came in."

"Very well, then. Good afternoon."

I figured out then who he reminded me of. With his overly polite demeanor, coupled with the air of violence and menace that hung around him, he was like the movie and TV gangsters played by Sheldon Leonard, the character actor and producer. I had a feeling Rafferty's civilized veneer was pretty thin.

Nobody followed us as we went down the stairs and back out through the security office and the casino. Ben Webster trudged along beside me without saying anything until we reached the deck.

Then he said quietly, "They really were cheating, you know. I'm not just a sore loser."

"I wouldn't know about that," I told him. "I wasn't there, and even if I had been, I don't know anything about how a roulette wheel could be rigged. I think you'd be smart to just let it go."

"What about the money I paid for a round-trip?"

I thought about it. Since he had brought the trouble down on himself, I figured I'd be within my rights to keep his money. But since I like to be accommodating, I said, "I'll refund you, say, thirty percent. But you'll have to wait and let me send you a check."

"I'll be out whatever a rental car costs me, too."

"Should've thought of that before you took a swing at that guy."

"Yeah, I guess so." He nodded, glum as ever. "All right. Thanks. I know you could've told me it was my own fault and to go to hell."

"That's right," I said. "I could have."

He stopped in front of a door with metal numerals 1 and 7 nailed to it. "This is my cabin."

"I'm sorry this happened. You'd better stay in there, like Mr. Rafferty told you. I got the feeling he was pretty mad. He'll call the cops if you give him any more trouble."

"He looked to me more like he wanted to break my neck."

"Yeah, well, he might do that, too."

I left Ben Webster at the door and headed back to my cabin. I got out my laptop and wrote an e-mail to Melissa, telling her to pull the file for Ben Webster and send a check for 30 percent of the money he had paid us to his home address. That was another big difference since Mark Twain's time: The riverboats hadn't been equipped with wireless Internet service back then. They didn't even have dial-up.

The cruise from St. Louis to Hannibal takes a couple of hours. The boat docks in Hannibal early enough so that folks can get some sightseeing done before dark. Then they have dinner on the boat and enjoy an evening of gambling and other entertainment, including Mark Lansing's performance as Mark Twain. More sightseeing the next morning rounds out the trip, and then the boat cruises back downriver to St. Louis that afternoon, so the whole trip takes about twenty-seven hours. That's long enough to give the passengers the authentic flavor of a Mississippi River voyage without causing a problem for modern-day attention spans.

I didn't have much interest in gambling. I own a small business; that's enough of a gamble for me. I didn't intend to spend the evening boozing it up like some of the passengers would, either. My hope was that nobody would get drunk and cause trouble. The incident with Ben Webster was more than enough of a ruckus for this trip.

So my plan was to take in the Mark Twain show in the salon. Mark Lansing had struck me as a nice guy, and I couldn't help but wonder what he looked like without the wig and the fake mustache and the old-man make-up.

I hoped the wild white hair and the big mustache really were fake. You never know, though, with actors. Some of them really get into the parts they play.

First, though, there were sights to see, and a little later, as the riverboat's steam whistle let out several shrill blasts, I knew we were about to dock at Hannibal, Missouri, boyhood home of Mr. Samuel Langhorne Clemens himself.

CHAPTER 3

I'd never been to Hannibal before. As I walked toward the front of the boat, I saw the town sprawled on the western bank of the river with rolling green hills behind it. Since tourism was an important industry here, it was deliberately picturesque. Oh, there were plenty of modern touches visible, but many of the buildings really were old and had been restored to look like they had in Mark Twain's time, like the riverboat itself.

Quite a few of the passengers had gathered on the bow to watch the approach to the dock. I saw about half the members of my group among them. The others were still in the casino, I supposed. I noticed Eddie and Louise Kramer at the railing. She was snapping pictures with a digital camera. I was sort of surprised to see that he wasn't talking on his cell phone but was resting his hands on the railing instead and looking at Hannibal with what appeared to be genuine interest. Maybe his wife had read him the riot

act about actually enjoying this vacation of
theirs, even though she didn't seem the type to
do such a thing.

I didn't see Ben Webster anywhere. I supposed he was still holed up in his cabin. That
was good. Once we docked he could come out
and get off the boat.

The whistle blew again. Several people strolled
out onto the dock and waved enthusiastically at
the passengers as the riverboat approached. The
women wore bonnets and long skirts and carried
parasols. The men were in old-fashioned suits
and beaver hats. One young couple wore the
sort of period clothing that youngsters would
have in Mark Twain's time. I knew from the Internet research I'd done before the trip that
they were supposed to be Tom Sawyer and
Becky Thatcher. Folks in Hannibal played up its
literary heritage for all it was worth, and I didn't
blame them a bit for doing so. The tourists
would have been disappointed if it wasn't that
way.

The captain, or whoever was at the wheel of
the *Southern Belle,* maneuvered the boat next to
the dock and brought it to a stop with a smooth,
graceful touch. The big paddlewheels on the
sides stopped turning. Water sluiced off the
paddles and sloshed against the pilings that sup-
ported the dock. Members of the crew hurried
to extend a railed gangway from the main deck
to the dock so that the passengers could disem-
bark.

I didn't have any group activities planned for
the afternoon or evening, although I had a

table reserved in the riverboat's dining room so anyone who wanted to eat together could. My clients were free to take in whatever sights they wanted to, and there were plenty of dinner theaters and restaurants in Hannibal where they could eat if they chose. Or they could continue gambling in the boat's casino if that was what they wanted to do. The more informal tours like this were welcome breaks from having to herd groups of tourists around from one attraction to another.

People began disembarking from the boat as soon as the gangway was in place, among them the Kramers. I lingered there along the rail, waiting to make sure that Ben Webster got off the boat. I could see the door to Cabin 17 from where I was and expected to see it open any minute now.

But it didn't.

I waited some more. Still no sign of Ben Webster. He couldn't have gotten off the boat without me seeing him, I thought. I'd been close to the gangway ever since the boat docked.

If Webster didn't leave, like Logan Rafferty had told him to, Rafferty might call the cops and have him arrested. That would lead to bad publicity for my tour. Webster seemed like a pretty good kid overall, so that was another reason to avoid bringing the law into this. I walked along the deck to Cabin 17 and knocked on the door.

No one answered. I knocked harder and called, "Mr. Webster!" When he still didn't respond I added, "This is Ms. Dickinson. We've docked at

Hannibal. You need to get off the boat now, Mr. Webster."

Nothing.

I was starting to get mad now. Rafferty had offered Webster a way to smooth this over with a minimum of fuss and no legal involvement. Sure, he'd lose a little money and have his trip ruined, but that was his own fault. Now, by refusing to come out of his cabin, he was causing more trouble for me.

Assuming, of course, that he was actually *in* his cabin, I suddenly thought. I hadn't been keeping an eye on Cabin 17 ever since the incident. He could have slipped out of it almost anytime. He could be anywhere on the boat's three decks by now. I didn't relish the idea of having to search the entire *Southern Belle* for him.

So much for him being a good kid. Maybe he really was a troublemaker.

I wanted to find him myself. I could go to Rafferty and get his security personnel involved in the search, but if I did that, Rafferty would likely call the police because Webster had reneged on the agreement to leave the boat. I wished Luke were here so I could split up the chore with him.

But he was back in Atlanta, so it was up to me to locate Ben Webster on my own. I started by making a circuit of the main deck.

This deck had passenger cabins, the casino, and the dining room. On the second deck were offices, the salon, and more passenger cabins. The third deck was off limits to passengers except for observation areas at bow and stern; crew quarters were up there, as well as more offices. The pilothouse that sat on the very top of the boat was off limits as well except for scheduled tours that let passengers see the river from the vantage point of the captain and the pilot.

It took me an hour to cover all the areas where passengers were permitted. Since Ben Webster was already in trouble, I figured it wasn't very likely he would venture into the off-limits areas. But nothing was impossible. If I didn't find him in any of the public areas, I'd have to consider asking Rafferty for help in searching the other parts of the boat.

When I had looked everywhere I could look and still hadn't found any trace of Ben Webster, I went back down to the main deck. I was getting pretty hot under the collar. I'd wanted to see some of the sights in Hannibal myself, and I couldn't do it as long as he was missing. This time I didn't just knock on the door of his cabin—I pounded on that sucker.

While I was doing that, somebody came up behind me and said, "Excuse me? Can I help you?"

I turned around to see a tall young man with blond hair standing there. He looked familiar, and I realized after a second that he was another member of the tour group. I had met him at the luncheon earlier that day. I'm usually pretty good with names, but I was upset enough right then that I couldn't come up with his.

He knew me, though. He smiled in recognition and went on, "Ms. Dickinson, right? I'm Vince Mallory. I'm a member of your tour."

"Of course, I remember you, Mr. Mallory," I

told him. "I was just looking for another member of the tour."

A slight frown of confusion appeared on his face. "Then, uh, why are you pounding on the door of my cabin like you're trying to knock it down?"

"Your cabin?" I blinked. "This isn't Ben Webster's cabin?"

"Who?"

"Ben Webster," I repeated. "About your age, six feet tall, dark hair . . ."

Vince Mallory was shaking his head before I finished describing Webster. He said, "I'm sorry, I don't know the guy. But I'm sure this is my cabin." He reached into the pocket of his jeans and brought out a key. "See, here's the key to this door."

He slipped the key into the lock, turned it, and sure enough, the door opened. I looked into the room. It was empty.

I closed my eyes for a second and told myself that I was a darned fool. I had walked off and left Ben Webster standing in front of the door like he was about to go in, but I hadn't actually seen him enter the cabin. He'd waited until I was gone, then headed for somewhere else on the boat!

"Is there a problem?" Vince Mallory asked.

"No, not at all," I lied. I had an unaccounted-for rogue tourist with a grudge, that was all. Ben Webster had to be hiding somewhere on the riverboat, and the only reason for him to do that would be if he wanted to cause trouble of some sort. To avenge his losses in the casino that he thought were caused by a rigged roulette wheel. To get back at Rafferty for threatening him. Heck, who knew what was going on in Ben Webster's mind. All I knew was that it couldn't be anything good.

"I'd be glad to give you a hand if there's anything I can do," Vince Mallory said.

"No, everything's fine," I said. I had thought of something else I could check. But first I forced myself back into tour director mode. "Are you heading into Hannibal to see some of the sights this afternoon?"

"Yeah, I thought I would. I've been in the casino, but you can't just gamble away the whole trip, now can you?" He waved a hand toward Hannibal. "Not with all this history waiting to be seen and experienced."

"You're a history buff, are you?"

"I had a double major in college: history and American literature. That was before I sort of got sidetracked into the military."

He had sort of a military look about him, all right. Probably the short hair and the fact that he was in really good shape. He didn't really seem like the academic type, but he went on, "Mark Twain has always been a particular interest of mine. When I was doing graduate work I planned to write my doctoral thesis on him."

"But you got sidetracked," I said.

He grinned. "Yeah. Wound up an MP instead of a PhD. Funny how life works out sometimes, isn't it?"

"It sure is. Are you still in the service?"

"No, I've been out for a while. I've been trying to decide whether to go back to school or maybe get into the security field."

He was a likable young guy, but I had a potential crisis on my hands. I had chatted long enough to do my duty as the tour director, so I said, "Well, I'll see you later, more than likely. Enjoy your cruise, Mr. Mallory."

"Thank you." He looked concerned. "You're sure there's nothing I can do to help you?"

"No, thanks." I smiled and turned to head for my cabin.

When I got there I opened my laptop and called up the records for this cruise. I had a copy of the passenger manifest that someone in Charles Gallister's office had e-mailed to me earlier in the day. In addition to giving me something to check against my own records, it provided the numbers of the cabins assigned to my clients. It took me only a second to scroll down the list to Ben Webster's name and see that he was supposed to be in Cabin 135.

That was on the second deck. The son of a gun had lied to me. He had picked Vince Mallory's cabin at random and claimed it was his so he could get away from me and do whatever it was he planned to do—which couldn't be anything good. Now I was stuck with not knowing where he was or what he was up to.

I still had one thing I could check before giving up and going to Rafferty, though. I left my cabin and hurried up to the second deck again. Earlier I had walked all around it looking for Webster, but I hadn't knocked on the door to Cabin 135. That's what I did now.

Somehow, I wasn't the least bit surprised when there was no answer.

I tried the knob, not expecting the door to be unlocked. But it was. I confess, I jumped a little in surprise when the knob turned in my hand. I didn't know whether to open the door or not. It had occurred suddenly to me that I might not like what I found in there.

But I had gone too far to back out now, I figured, so I eased the door open a couple of inches and knocked on it again, just in case. I even called out, "Mr. Webster? Ben? Are you in there?"

When there was no answer, I really thought about closing the door and going for help, so I wouldn't have to go in there by myself. I sort of wished now that I'd asked Vince Mallory to come with me. Having a big, strapping former MP with me would have done wonders for my confidence right then.

It seemed like I stood there, torn by indecision, a lot longer than I actually did. Probably not more than a couple of seconds went by after I called out before I pushed the door all the way open and stepped into the cabin with my heart pounding.

Nobody was in there.

Unless they were in the bathroom, my nervous brain reminded me. The closed door loomed ominously in a corner of the room.

I took a better look around first. There had been a suitcase sitting on the bed in Vince Mallory's cabin, as there probably was in most of the passenger cabins on the boat. Not here,

though. I didn't see a bag anywhere. I opened the
door to the tiny closet. No suitcase, no clothes
hanging up, nothing. By the looks of the cabin, it
could have been unoccupied.

That left the bathroom. There's an old saying
in the South about being as nervous as a cat on
a porch full of rocking chairs. That's how I felt
as I approached the bathroom door. I was ready
to jump.

I knocked on it first. "Mr. Webster? Are you in
there?"

Either he wasn't, or he couldn't answer.

"Stop that," I told myself out loud as that
thought went through my head. "Just because
you found a dead body that other time doesn't
mean you're gonna find one now."

I knew that made sense, but I still felt a whole
cloud of butterflies in my stomach as I reached
out and grasped the knob. I swallowed hard and
then turned it. I pushed the door open, halfway
expecting to bump up against a corpse.

Instead the door opened all the way, revealing a bathroom with a toilet, a tiny vanity, and a
shower, just like the one in my cabin. The
shower curtain was pulled across the opening. I
started to push it back, then hesitated. I didn't
think the shower was big enough for a body to
be hidden in it. The only way that would be possible would be if the body was stiff enough so it
could be propped up against the wall and stay
there.

With a rasp of curtain rings on the rod, I
shoved the curtain back.

Then blew out a long breath because the

shower was empty. Not just empty, but also dry, as if no one had used it since the passengers came on board.

I looked around the bathroom. It didn't take long. No shaving kit or anything else personal. The hand towel beside the vanity was damp, the only sign that this cabin had been occupied anytime recently. If not for that, it would have been like Ben Webster had never been here.

So he had come to his cabin and cleaned it out after leaving me down on the main deck, I thought. Why? It made sense if he'd been planning to get off the boat at Hannibal, as he'd agreed to do. But he hadn't gotten off. At least, I hadn't seen him if he had.

So where the heck was my missing tourist?

CHAPTER 4

I admit, I should have gone to Logan Rafferty, told him what was going on, and enlisted the help of him and his security personnel to find out what had happened to Ben Webster. But as I stood there in the empty cabin, I talked myself out of it, at least for the time being. I didn't *know* that anything had happened to Webster, just like I didn't *know* he was hiding somewhere and plotting to cause trouble. Either of those things was possible, but so were other explanations. He might have gotten off the riverboat, like he was supposed to, and I had just flat missed it. He also could have disembarked while I was wandering around the boat looking for him.

Don't borrow trouble, I told myself. I could tell from the response I'd gotten when I announced this tour that it was going to be popular. I didn't want to have future tours banned from the *Southern Belle*.

So, smart or not, I left Ben Webster's cabin

just like I found it, with the shower curtain pulled closed, the bathroom door shut, and the cabin door unlocked. I went out on deck, leaned on the railing, and looked at Hannibal while I thought about my next move. I had a good view from the second deck like this. The only ones better would be from the observation areas on the third deck or the pilothouse.

The crowds around the dock had thinned out. The tourists who had gotten off the boat had already spread out through the town. The locals in costume who had come out to greet them were gone, too, having lured customers back to whatever theater or museum employed them. A few stragglers might get tired of gambling or run out of money and decide to see the attractions that Hannibal offered, but for the most part everybody who was going to town was already there.

The more I thought about it, the more I believed that the most likely explanation was that Webster had gotten off the boat without me seeing him. His cabin looked like he had cleaned it out and left. I didn't know why he claimed that Vince Mallory's cabin was his. Maybe he had planned to pull some sort of angry stunt but later changed his mind. I doubted that he could have been wandering around the off-limits areas on the riverboat for this long without being caught by some of the crew. In that case, they would have turned him over to Logan Rafferty, who would have sent for me.

So when I thought about it like that, it

seemed obvious that Webster must have gotten off the boat. If I could just *prove* that, then I could relax and enjoy the rest of the tour, provided that no more problems cropped up.

There couldn't be that many rental car agencies in Hannibal, I told myself as I headed down the stairs to the main deck. All I had to do was find the one where Ben Webster had picked up a car to drive back to St. Louis.

I left the boat, walked off the dock, and headed up Center Street. When I got to Main I found myself at the Hannibal Trolley Company, which operated sightseeing trolleys around the town. I thought they might be able to tell me where the nearest car rental agencies were, or at least have a phone book I could look at.

The folks at the trolley company were friendly. No surprise there, in a town that catered so much to the tourist trade. The lady working at the counter pointed me to the car rental places, adding, "But why rent a car when our trolleys can take you anywhere in Hannibal you want to go?"

I told her I was just looking for some information and headed for the nearest car rental agency.

It took me the better part of an hour to hike around Hannibal to all the places where Ben Webster could have rented a car. My frustration grew right along with the tired ache in my legs. The folks at the agencies were all cooperative—they could have refused to answer my questions, after all—but none of them recalled renting a car to anybody who looked like Webster that afternoon, and his name didn't show up in their records.

So if he wasn't on the boat and he hadn't rented a car to drive back to St. Louis, where was he?

I pondered that question as I started retracing my steps toward the river. My route took me past the Mark Twain Boyhood Home and Museum, at the corner of Main and Hill streets. Hill Street, as you might guess, was kind of steep. The narrow, two-story white frame building where Sam Clemens had grown up faced the street with an old stone building sitting hard against it on the left side. A sign identified the stone building as the Mark Twain Museum and Gift Shop. Across the street sat another white frame structure known as the Becky Thatcher House. I knew from my research for the tour that young Sam Clemens's childhood playmate Laura Hawkins, later immortalized in *The Adventures of Tom Sawyer* under the name Becky Thatcher, had lived there.

That was interesting, but it didn't help me find out where Ben Webster had gone. Maybe he was wandering around Hannibal trying to see some of the sights, at least, before renting a car and heading back to St. Louis. I started into the boyhood home, thinking how ironic it would be if I ran smack-dab into Webster after searching for him all over the boat and hiking over half of downtown Hannibal.

I didn't see Ben Webster anywhere in the house, but the Kramers were there. Louise greeted me with a smile. Eddie just grunted and gave me a curt nod.

"This is all so fascinating," Louise gushed. "I just love Mark Twain, don't you?"

"Sure," I said. To tell the truth, I'd read *Tom Sawyer* and *Huck Finn* in school, like everybody else, and I wasn't sure I'd ever picked up anything by Twain since then. I sure as heck couldn't have written a thesis on him and his work like Vince Mallory had talked about doing.

But the people who had signed up for the tour didn't have to know that. I'd done enough research on Twain so I could talk about him with enough enthusiasm and knowledge to satisfy most people with a casual interest in him.

"I'm really looking forward to the performance on the boat tonight," Louise went on. "That man who plays Mark Twain looks just like him, don't you think?"

I agreed that Mark Lansing bore a strong resemblance to the man he portrayed. "I plan to be there, too," I told Louise, remembering the promise I had made earlier that afternoon. I hoped nothing interfered with that plan.

I didn't expect anything serious to come of it, since I'd be back in Atlanta in another day or two, but I wouldn't mind spending some more time in Mark Lansing's company. Will Burke and I dated fairly often, but we hadn't gotten to the point where either of us wanted the relationship to be exclusive. Heck, after having a twenty-year-plus marriage end in divorce, I wasn't sure I *ever* wanted anything that committed again.

I left Louise Kramer poring over the furnishings in the boyhood home and her husband Eddie looking bored. My next stop was the museum and gift shop next door. I described Ben Webster to the clerks behind the counter in the gift shop, but none of them remembered seeing him.

"But we have so many people coming through here, you know," one of the women said with an apologetic shrug.

"I know y'all do," I told her. "I appreciate your help anyway."

While I was there I took a quick walk through the museum. Under other circumstances, I might have enjoyed it, but worrying over the Webster situation kept me from concentrating on what I was looking at. After a few minutes I gave up on trying to see the sights for myself and headed across the street to the Becky Thatcher House.

There was a gift shop there, too, but that clerk didn't remember Webster, either. The same thing was true at the nearby Twain Interpretive Center and the restored building that had served as the office of Sam Clemens's father when he was justice of the peace in Hannibal. No one recalled seeing Webster, but because of the amount of tourists that came through all these attractions, nobody could be sure.

It was time to give up, I told myself. I had done what I could. But even though I knew that was true, logically, worry nibbled at my brain as I walked back to the riverboat. Dusk was settling down over the town. It was going to be a warm night, and we were far enough from St. Louis that the air was fairly clean, without the sort of pollution you get in a big city. Having lived in Atlanta as long as I had, even relatively clean air tasted a little like wine when you took a deep breath of it. I should have been enjoying this gorgeous early evening, instead of worrying.

Tell that to my nerves. They were as tight as piano wires as I went back on board.

A reception was scheduled in the salon before dinner. People could come and go as they pleased, of course, but I expected a fairly good turnout. I went to my cabin and traded my slacks, blouse, and blazer for a simple dark blue dress that I thought looked elegant without being flashy. Low heels replaced the comfortable walking shoes I'd been wearing earlier as I tramped around Hannibal. I ran my fingers through my short red hair to fluff it out. I thought I looked good enough to sip a little champagne at the reception and then eat dinner.

A few of my clients were already in the salon when I got there. I greeted them and asked them how the tour was going for them so far. Everybody seemed to be having a good time. I started to relax, telling myself that the whole business with Ben Webster would blow over without any more trouble. Sure, I didn't know where he was, but he was a grown-up and it wasn't my job to keep track of his every move. As long as he wasn't on the boat, his whereabouts weren't any of my business anymore.

I became aware that a man sitting at the bar was watching me. Not to be vain about it or any-thing, but I've had a few men eye me in bars over the years. Not as many as when I was younger, maybe, but it still happened. This man wore jeans and a sports jacket and had dark blond hair over a pleasantly rugged face. When I caught him looking at me, he didn't jerk his eyes away or look guilty. He just gave me a friendly smile and lifted the glass in his hand like he was saluting me.

That interested me enough that I went over to him. "Hello," I said. "Have we met?"

"We have, Ms. Dickinson," he said.

"I'm sorry. Normally I remember ruggedly handsome men—"

"And I always remember pretty redheads." His voice changed, took on a slight quiver like that of an older man. "I quite fancy redheaded women, you know."

"Well, Mark Twain, as I live and breathe!"

Mark Lansing grinned. "That's right. You didn't recognize me at all without the wig and the mus-tache and the make-up, did you?"

"No, you look totally different," I told him. "Bigger, even."

"That's a trick. You stoop over a little and draw your shoulders forward, and people think you're smaller than you really are."

"What are you doing here? I'm surprised to see you out of costume. It must take a long time to get ready, and you've got a performance tonight." I checked my watch. "In a little more than two hours, in fact."

"It only takes about thirty minutes to get the make-up and the mustache on," he said with a shrug. "The wig and the clothes take only a few minutes. I can't wear the getup all the time. It'd drive me nuts. I'd rather take the time and trouble to take it off and put it back on every now and then."

"Well, I reckon I can understand that. Pretendin' is fun, but deep down everybody wants to be who they really are."

"Pretty profound for a redhead."

I gave him a mock glare. "The last fella who said something like that to me got pitched overboard."

"How about if I buy you a drink to make up for it?"

"I think you just wanted an excuse to buy me a drink."

He grinned again. "Now that you mention it . . ."

"Champagne," I said to the bartender.

"Ouch," Mark Lansing said.

I ignored him and went on, "I'm Delilah Dickinson."

"Yes, ma'am;" the bartender said. "I'll fetch the bottle I've been using for your party."

"What, I'm not paying?" Mark asked.

"And give a glass to my friend here," I told the bartender.

"Yes, ma'am."

Mark shook his head. "Great, now I feel like a gigolo."

"Shut up and drink your champagne," I said.

It felt good to relax and flirt with a good-looking man for a few minutes. That's all it was, just some harmless flirting, but I was glad that I'd run into Mark Lansing without his Mark Twain garb on.

We sipped champagne and talked a while longer, the sort of small talk that a man and a woman make when they think they might be interested in each other and want to get to know each other better. I mentioned my divorce but didn't go into detail about it. He said that he'd never been married but had come close a couple of times.

"Cold feet?" I asked.

"Jobs got in the way," he said. "I'm attracted to successful women, I guess. The ones I was thinking about asking to marry me got good job offers on the other side of the country. I didn't want to leave St. Louis, and I wasn't going to ask them to turn down the jobs because of me."

"You're from St. Louis?"

"Yeah. Actually I was born in a little town down in the boot heel of Missouri, but I was raised in St. Louis."

"Have you been acting long?"

"No, not really. The bug bit me late."

"What did you do before that?"

He shrugged. "I was a lawyer."

I tried not to stare at him. "Let me get this straight. You gave up being a lawyer so you could play Mark Twain for a bunch of tourists on a riverboat?"

"Yeah, pretty crazy, isn't it?" he asked with a grin. "But there comes a time when you've got to do what you want in life, or what's the point?"

I couldn't argue with that.

"What about you?" he went on. "Did you always want to be a travel agent?"

"Well . . . not really. But once I got into the business, I liked it." I told him about working for one of the big agencies in Atlanta until I finally decided to take that leap of faith and open my own business. As I told him, I saw that he had done basically the same thing by leaving law and becoming an actor. That was a leap of faith, too.

I went on to tell him about my daughter, Melissa, and her husband, Luke, and my twin teenage nieces, Augusta and Amelia. I didn't tell him anything about what had happened during the first *Gone With the Wind* tour the year before. I didn't want to scare him off.

Both of us lost track of the time for a while, a sign that we were enjoying the conversation. Eventually Mark glanced at his watch and said, "I've got to go get ready for the performance. Maybe we can talk some more afterward."

"I'd like that," I told him.

He left the salon. I checked the time myself and saw that I was almost too late for dinner. I had forgotten all about it while I was talking to Mark. With a wave to the bartender, I left the salon.

Most of my clients who planned to have dinner on the boat had probably eaten already, I thought as I headed down the stairs to the main deck. But a few of them might still be in the dining room, so I headed that way, figuring I could at least put in an appearance and maybe get something to eat. Just something to tide me over, though, because I was already thinking about suggesting a late supper to Mark. . . .

The sobs coming from a dark area along the rail caught my attention and made me freeze. I didn't know who was there. All I could see was a shadowy figure bending over the railing. I thought about going to find a steward, but that seemed a little cowardly. Instead I said, "Hello? Is there something I can do for you?"

The figure jerked around from the rail and came at me.

CHAPTER 5

I started to jump back and raise my arms to defend myself, but then I recognized Louise Kramer. I couldn't bring myself to believe that the meek little woman was attacking me, so I stayed where I was. Sure enough, Louise didn't do anything except hug me and get the shoulder of my dress wet where her tears were falling.

"Why, honey," I managed to say, "what in the world is wrong?"

She shook her head and didn't answer. I patted her on the back and made the sort of vaguely comforting noises that people always do in situations like that.

Then a possible explanation occurred to me. I said, "Did that big ol' husband of yours do something? Did he hurt you, Louise?" My blood started to boil at the thought.

That finally jolted her out of her teary silence. "What? You mean Eddie? Oh, no! Eddie would . . . would never hurt me."

I wasn't so sure about that. I hadn't liked the

look of Eddie Kramer earlier in the day. He was nearly twice the size of his wife, and from the sound of the way he'd talked to whoever was on the phone, he liked to bully people. Size and meanness were a bad combination.

"Are you sure? I can call somebody, or go find a security officer—"

She jerked away from me. "No! I told you, Eddie didn't do anything to me. I . . . I'm just upset. It's personal. There's nothing you can do to help."

One thing I've learned in the travel business is your clients' personal lives really aren't any of your business. As long as they don't disrupt the tour or break any laws, you're better off giving them their privacy.

That's what I did then, backing off and holding up my hands. "I'm sorry," I told Louise. "Whatever's wrong, I didn't mean to intrude. But I meant it when I said that if there's anything I can do, I'd like to help."

She took a handkerchief or a tissue from her purse. In the dim light, I couldn't tell which. She used it to dab at her eyes and then took a deep breath, composing herself with a visible effort.

"Thank you, Ms. Dickinson."

"Delilah."

She summoned up a smile. "Delilah. I promise you, there's nothing you can do. I'll be all right in a little while."

"Well . . . okay. If you're sure."

"I'm certain."

My eyes were more used to the dim light now. I could see that she didn't have any bruises or black eyes or anything like that. Nothing visible, anyway. And she had sounded like she was telling the truth when she said that her husband hadn't hurt her. I knew I should have been ashamed of myself for jumping to that conclusion, but I wasn't. Not after I'd seen the way some women were treated in their marriages.

"I was just on my way to the dining room to see if there's anything left to eat," I told her. "If you haven't had dinner yet, why don't you join me?"

"Oh, I . . . I couldn't eat anything right now. But thank you for asking. I . . . I think I'll go back to my cabin and lie down for a little while."

"You're comin' to the salon for the Mark Twain performance, aren't you?"

"I'll try," she said with a weak smile, but I didn't honestly believe that I'd see her there.

She walked toward her cabin—or toward what I hoped was really her cabin, after the trick Ben Webster had pulled on me earlier. I didn't think Louise Kramer had any reason to try to fool me. I watched, anyway, as she took a key from her purse, unlocked a cabin door, went inside, and shut the door softly behind her. She struck me as the sort of woman who had never slammed a door in her life.

That was an odd little incident, I thought as I started toward the dining room again, but it wasn't that uncommon for somebody to get emotional and lose control momentarily while on a vacation. Traveling was really stressful for some people, after all.

More of my clients than I expected were still

in the dining room when I got there. I helped myself to some appetizers at the buffet table and then circulated among the guests, asking them how they were enjoying the trip so far and things like that. Just pleasant chitchat.

I mentioned the Mark Twain performance in the salon to everyone, too, urging them to attend. I wanted Mark Lansing to have a good crowd for his first performance, although, when I stopped to think about it, he might have preferred not to have so many people looking at him. I knew that if I were an actor or a singer or something like that, the bigger the crowd, the more butterflies I'd have fluttering around in my stomach.

But it was too late to do anything about that now. Quite a few people expressed an interest in watching the performance, so as the time approached eight o'clock, I led a good-sized group out of the dining room and up the stairs to the second deck. We went into the salon and found places to sit at the bar and at the tables, and there were comfortable chairs and divans scattered around the sumptuously furnished room.

I didn't see Eddie or Louise Kramer anywhere in the salon, but that didn't surprise me, even though I was a little disappointed. I'd been hoping that Louise would feel better and would want to take in the show.

A few minutes later, the double doors from the deck opened, and Mark Twain ambled in, cigar in hand. He went to the bar, rested an elbow on it, and looked around the room at the passengers, who had quieted down as he made his way across the salon. Once everyone was quiet, he said, "Man is the only animal that blushes. Or needs to."

That got a nice laugh. Mark acknowledged it with a wave of the unlit cigar. "I want to welcome all of you to the *Southern Belle*. As some of you may be aware, I worked on riverboats much like this one, back in my early days. I was an apprentice pilot to Captain Horace Bixby, whose task it was to teach me the river. But the face of the water itself, in time, became a wonderful book . . . a book that was a dead language to the uneducated passenger, but which told its mind to me without reserve, delivering its most cherished secrets as clearly as if it uttered them with a voice. And it was not a book to be read once and thrown aside, for it had a new story to tell every day."

I guessed that most of that must have been a passage from *Life on the Mississippi* that Mark Lansing had memorized. He continued talking in Twain's words about the river, about how the slightest ripple might indicate a snag under the water that could tear the bottom right out of a riverboat. Despite its peaceful, placid appearance, the river hid many dangers under its slow-moving surface, and a good pilot had to be able to recognize all of them instinctively.

Mark was good; I had to give him that. He spoke Twain's words with precision and conviction. After a while, listening to him was like being back there roughly a hundred and fifty years earlier, when the country was still young and brawling and vibrant.

Gradually the focus shifted from the river to young Sam Clemens's boyhood in Hannibal. I didn't know which pieces of writing the passages came from—probably more than one—but Mark wove them together into a narrative that was, well, rollicking. It was easy to see how young Sam's experiences in Hannibal had become the stuff of fiction in *The Adventures of Tom Sawyer* and *Adventures of Huckleberry Finn.* Mark kept the audience alternating between rapt attention and uproarious laughter. He never broke character and was never less than convincing in his portrayal.

Most of the performance had to do with Hannibal and the Mississippi, but to wrap it up Mark performed some material about Twain's days as a newspaper correspondent in the West, then talked about politics for a while. The jabs at Congress and the president were as timely as when Twain wrote them, and the passengers in the salon seemed to enjoy them a lot. When Mark waved his cigar in the air and said, "Good evening, ladies and gentlemen," they gave him a standing ovation.

After the performance people crowded around to talk to him. Some of them even wanted an autograph, which Mark provided even though he looked a little uncomfortable doing so. I thought he did, anyway. He stayed in character while chatting with the passengers. I waited until they left him alone before I slipped up beside him.

"Oh, Mr. Twain, that was just amazin'," I said

in a breathless voice. "You're my favorite writer in the whole wide world."

Mark kept smiling under the bushy mustache, but he said, "I don't think I've ever been so scared in my whole life."

"You didn't have anything to be scared about. You were great!"

"You really think so?"

I nodded and said, "I do."

"You're not just saying that?"

"Nope. You had all these folks eatin' right out of the palm of your hand. I think everybody in here enjoyed it. I know I did."

"Well, it's kind of you to say so." Mark took a handkerchief from the breast pocket of the white suit coat he wore and patted his forehead with it. A little make-up came off on the handkerchief.

I linked my arm with his and said, "Come on over to the bar. It's not every day I can ask Mark Twain to have a drink with me."

The same bartender brought us champagne. Mark had some trouble drinking his through the drooping fake mustache, but he managed. "Next time I'll get rid of this soup strainer first," he complained.

"No, no, you have to leave it on," I told him. "It makes you look distinguished."

"You really think it went all right?"

"I know it did."

Mark relaxed after that, and we chatted about his performance and the passengers' reactions. Some of them still came up to him to shake his hand and thank him for an entertaining evening. He seemed to enjoy talking to them, and after a while I leaned over to him and said, "I think you may have a future in this business."

"What, riverboat acting?"

"It's a start. Today, the riverboat. Tomorrow, Hollywood or Broadway!"

"Let's not get ahead of ourselves," he cautioned, but I could tell he was pleased by what I'd said.

I started thinking about what a pleasant evening it had turned out to be after all, despite the strains and worries of the afternoon. The Kramers could work out their problems between themselves. Wherever Ben Webster had gone, at least I was confident he wasn't still on the riverboat. The rest of the overnight cruise was bound to go smoothly.

I know, I know. I'm dumb that way sometimes.

I was nursing another glass of champagne when the cell phone in my purse rang. Thinking that it might be Melissa or Luke, I said, "Excuse me a minute," to Mark and stepped away from the bar while I took the phone from my purse.

The number on the display wasn't a familiar one, though. I didn't even recognize the area code. I opened the phone and said, "Delilah Dickinson."

"Ms. Dickinson." It was a man's voice, calm and powerful, and one that I'd never heard before, as far as I could recall. I didn't have to wonder whom it belonged to, though, because he went on immediately, "This is Captain Williams."

"Captain Williams?" I repeated.

"Captain of the *Southern Belle*," he explained. "Where are you right now?"

The blunt question took me by surprise. "Why, I'm in the salon—" I began.

"Stay right there if you would, please. Mr. Rafferty will come and get you."

"Come and . . . get me?" Whatever this was, if Rafferty was involved it couldn't be good.

"That's right. There's something . . . or rather, someone . . . you need to see."

No, sir, I thought. Not good at all.

CHAPTER 6

Mark must have seen the worried look on my face as I closed my cell phone and slipped it back into my purse. "Problem?" he asked. "Something about your tour?"

"I don't know." I picked up my glass and threw back the rest of the champagne. Luckily there wasn't much of it left, or I might have choked on it. "That was Captain Williams. You know him?"

"I've met him a couple of times. I'm new at the job of playing Mark Twain, remember? I don't know any of the crew all that well yet."

"When you talked to him, did the captain strike you as the sort of fella who'd get worked up over something if it wasn't important?"

"Not at all," Mark said, not hesitating a bit. "He seemed very calm and levelheaded to me."

There went my idea that maybe the captain wanted to fuss at me because one of my clients littered the deck or something like that. Calm and levelheaded meant that Williams wouldn't be sending the head of security to fetch me unless something important had happened.

"If there's anything I can do to help . . ." Mark went on.

I didn't want to burden him with my problems. Besides, I didn't even know yet what the problem was. So I shook my head and said, "No, that's all right. But I appreciate the offer from a famous man like Mark Twain."

Just then, Logan Rafferty came into the salon. He moved with a brisk efficiency that said while he wasn't hurrying, he wasn't wasting any time, either. He spotted me and started across the salon toward me.

I put my hand on the sleeve of Mark's white coat for a second and said, "Maybe I'll see you later. Congratulations again on your performance."

Rafferty wore a pretty grim expression as I went to meet him. "Ms. Dickinson," he said. "Please come with me."

He kept his voice pitched low. I could tell that he didn't want to attract any more attention than he had to. That was sort of difficult to do, though, as big and tough-looking as he was.

"Where are we going?" I asked as we started toward the door of the salon.

"Captain Williams will explain everything to you." He paused, then added, "And you've got some explaining to do, too."

"Hey, I may be a redhead, but I'm not Lucy Ricardo."

He didn't as much as grunt. I don't know if he didn't get the reference, or if he just didn't have much of a sense of humor. Of course, the comment wasn't really that funny to begin with, I told myself.

I expected Rafferty to take me up to the pilot-house, since that's where Captain Williams would normally be. Instead, when we reached the stairway, he headed down toward the main deck. But he didn't stop there. He opened a door and revealed some stairs that led below decks. Down there was the belly of the boat, the engine room and the boilers and all the other things that made the *Southern Belle* go.

"Where are we going?" I asked, suddenly feeling even more nervous than I was before. "Are you sure Captain Williams is down here?"

"He's waiting for us," Rafferty said.

Short of turning and running, which he hadn't really given me any reason to do, my only other option seemed to be to follow him down those stairs. With plenty of misgivings, I did so.

Since the boat was docked, the main engines were off, but I could still hear the rumble of the generators that provided electricity. The riverboats in Mark Twain's time hadn't been equipped like that, of course, but there were only so many creature comforts modern tourists would give up in the name of authenticity. Folks wanted to be able to flip a switch and have lights and air-conditioning.

When we reached the bottom of the stairs, Rafferty led me along a narrow, metal-walled corridor. We turned a couple of times and then went around a corner to see several men standing in front of a small door set into the wall.

The door was partially open, but I couldn't see through it because of the man who stood in front of it.

He was tall and slender—lean was actually more like it—and wore a white uniform with gold braid on it. A black cap sat on his head. He was in his sixties, I estimated, based on his white hair and the weathered look of his face. Dark eyes stabbed at me as he snapped, "Ms. Dickinson?"

I recognized his voice. "Captain?"

"That's right. I'm Captain L. B. Williams. You're the head of Dickinson Literary Tours?"

"Yes, sir, I am. If you don't mind, can I ask what this is all about?"

Evidently I couldn't, because he didn't answer me. Instead he asked another question of his own.

"A man named Ben Webster booked passage on the *Southern Belle* through your agency?"

"That's right."

"I'm sorry to have to tell you this, Ms. Dickinson, but Mr. Webster is dead."

In the back of my mind, I'd been halfway expecting that. The other half had been worried that Webster had done something to damage the boat. So I felt both relief and shock, mostly shock, at the news he was dead.

Then it was all shock as Captain Williams stepped aside so that I could see through the partially open door into what was evidently a storage closet of some sort. The only thing stored in there now was a body. Somebody had crammed Ben Webster into the locker, doubling up his arms and legs so that he would fit. No way he could have gotten in there like that himself, I thought.

He hadn't broken his own neck, either. I could tell by the odd angle of his head that his neck was broken. He hadn't committed suicide. He hadn't tried to hide in the locker and accidentally killed himself.

No, Ben Webster had been murdered, sure as anything, I thought.

"You seem to be taking this awfully calmly, Ms. Dickinson," Williams commented. "Did you already know that Mr. Webster was dead?"

I opened my mouth to tell him that no, the only reason I was able to handle this catastrophe without falling apart was that I had a little experience with murder, from the time Luke and I took a tour group to the plantation.

But I never got the words out, because it suddenly didn't matter that I had seen murder victims before. I hadn't seen *this* murder victim. I hadn't looked into Ben Webster's wide, staring eyes that no longer saw anything, or noted that the tip of his tongue stuck out a little between his lips, or thought about how, if rigor mortis had already set in, whoever took him out of the locker might have to break his arms and legs just to straighten him out again. All of that was new, and it was too much.

I felt my eyes rolling up in their sockets and was aware that I was falling backward. That was all I knew before I passed out.

*   *   *

When I came to and opened my eyes, Captain Williams had taken off his captain's cap and was fanning my face with it. I was lying on something soft, and I had to squint against the breeze Williams was stirring up and tilt my head to see that I was lying in Logan Rafferty's lap.

I let out a yelp and started trying to struggle into a sitting position. "Get off me!" I said to Rafferty.

"You're mixed up, Ms. Dickinson," he said. "I believe you're the one on me."

"Yeah, but I was unconscious! That's the only way I'd ever be anywhere near your lap, you . . . you . . ."

While I was sputtering in indignation, Captain Williams said, "Are you all right, Ms. Dickinson?"

"I just fainted, that's all." Too much champagne and not enough food, I thought. That, and the sight of a corpse crammed into a storage locker.

"You didn't hit your head when you fell, or anything like that?"

I had managed to sit up. I tugged my dress down with one hand and patted my head with the other, feeling for any goose eggs. I didn't find any.

"I'm fine," I said. "At least I will be if one of you *gentlemen* will help me up."

Two of the three other men standing in the corridor wore white trousers and dark blue shirts. That was the uniform the stewards and other crew members wore. The third man was in khaki work clothes. The grease stains on his hands told me he probably tended the engines.

Rafferty had stood up. He took my hand and lifted me to my feet. Instinctively, I brushed myself off, even though the corridor floor seemed pretty clean.

"I apologize," Williams said. "I admit that I intended to shock you by showing you Webster's body, Ms. Dickinson. I thought that if you knew anything about his death, you might blurt it out."

I glanced at Rafferty. "Sounds like something *you* would do."

He held up his hands and shook his head. "The captain's running this show. He's the final authority on this boat."

"Well, within reason," Williams said. "I'm afraid that in circumstances such as these, I'll have to defer to the law. Call the Hannibal police, Mr. Rafferty."

Rafferty hesitated. "We don't know when or where Webster was killed. If it was while we were still on the river, before we docked, the State Police will have jurisdiction."

That answered my question about who was responsible for law enforcement on the Mississippi, I thought.

"We'll start by notifying the authorities in Hannibal," Williams decided. "If they want to, they can call in the State Police."

Rafferty shrugged, took out his cell phone, and walked off down the corridor to make the call.

The captain's plan sounded logical to me. Let the cops sort it all out and decide what to do next. Whoever was in charge of the investigation, I intended to cooperate fully with them.

Which meant I'd have to tell them that Ben Webster had had a run-in earlier in the day with Logan Rafferty. I glanced at Rafferty from the corner of my eye.

He was big enough to break somebody's neck, that was for sure. He was considerably taller and heavier than Webster, and in his job as head of security for the riverboat, he'd probably had some training in handling passengers who had lost their temper and gotten violent, as well as practical experience. I didn't doubt for a second that he was capable of killing Ben Webster, at least physically.

I wasn't sure why he would have done such a thing, though. He had seemed satisfied with telling Webster he had to get off the boat when it docked in Hannibal.

But what if Webster had tried to cause more trouble after fooling me with that cabin trick? If Rafferty had caught him in the middle of committing some sort of sabotage, and the two of them had struggled . . .

It seemed reasonable to me. The problem was that if such a thing had happened, Rafferty could have just told the truth about it. It was his job to protect the *Southern Belle*, after all. He wouldn't have needed to hide Webster's body and try to cover up what had happened. There would have been an investigation, of course, and the incident might have hurt the riverboat's reputation and gotten Rafferty in trouble with the owner, Charles Gallister, but I was convinced

that he wouldn't have been charged with anything if things had happened according to the
scenario I laid out in my head.

Somebody else would have to sort that out.
There was also the operator of the roulette
wheel to consider. Webster had accused him of
cheating and taken a swing at him. However, I
thought it was pretty unlikely the fella would
have tracked Webster down later and killed him
over that.

As those thoughts were going through my
head, Captain Williams turned to me and asked,
"When was the last time you saw Mr. Webster?"

"Earlier this afternoon." I hesitated.

"Mr. Rafferty has told me about the incident
in the casino involving Mr. Webster," Williams
said. "You don't have to worry about revealing
anything you shouldn't."

"Well, in that case, it was right after that when
I saw Webster last. I went with him back to his
cabin and told him to get his things together so
he could leave the boat when it docked here in
Hannibal."

I didn't say anything about the cabin
switcheroo Webster had pulled. For one thing,
it made me look sort of dumb, and for another,
despite being the captain of the riverboat,
Williams wasn't a police officer. I didn't have to
answer his questions.

The trick about the cabins indicated to me
that Webster had been up to *something*, so I knew
I'd have to tell the cops about it. Until that time
came, I intended to keep that bit of information
to myself.

"Did he have any trouble with any of the other members of your tour group?"

That was the sort of question the cops would ask, too. But I could answer it honestly by shaking my head and saying, "Not that I know of." I asked a question of my own. "Who found Webster's body?"

Williams nodded toward the man in khakis and grease stains. "Henry here. He's one of our engineers."

I looked at the man and asked, "Is this some sort of storage closet?"

"That's right, ma'am," he answered. "We keep mostly tools in it. I opened the door to get a wrench I needed to adjust one of the valves on the boilers."

I forced myself to look into the closet again and saw that Webster's body had been shoved up against shelves that contained wrenches, hammers, screwdrivers, plastic boxes full of assorted nuts and bolts and washers, and a lot of other stuff that I didn't know what it was.

"Do you have to get things out of here pretty often?" I asked.

Henry shrugged and shook his head. "Not really. We keep the engines and boilers in topnotch shape, so they don't need much work except for routine maintenance, and all that's done while the boat's docked in St. Louis. It's not unusual for us to make several cruises without anybody ever having to open this door."

If someone knew that, they would also know that the supply closet wasn't a bad place to stash a body. There was at least a chance no one would discover it until the *Southern Belle* returned to St. Louis. To me, that seemed to indicate that the killer was somebody pretty familiar with the operation of the riverboat.

Like Logan Rafferty, I thought as the man himself came back along the corridor.

"The cops will be here in a few minutes," he announced.

Captain Williams frowned at me. "I didn't care for the tone of those questions you were asking, Ms. Dickinson," he said. "You seem to think that a member of my crew could be responsible for what happened to Mr. Webster."

"Well, you've got to admit it's a possibility," I said. "Shoot, right now everybody on the boat's a suspect, isn't that right?"

"There are close to a hundred passengers on board," Williams said, his voice cool. "Webster was a passenger. I'd say that's where you'll find the killer."

"*I* don't plan on findin' the killer," I said. "That's a job for the police."

And I sure hoped that it worked out that way this time.

CHAPTER 7

As Rafferty had predicted, it didn't take long for the cops to show up. Captain Williams sent one of the crew members up to the main deck to wait for them to arrive and bring them down here. The steward came back a few minutes later with a woman in plainclothes and two uniformed men following him.

The woman took the lead, saying, "Captain Williams? I'm Detective Charlotte Travis from the Hannibal Police Department."

She was a few years younger than me, around thirty-five, I guessed. Thick blond hair hung to her shoulders. She was pretty but didn't try to make anything out of it. That wouldn't stop men from looking at her appreciatively, though. Rafferty sure did.

Williams shook hands with her and introduced himself. "Captain L. B. Williams, Detective. This is my head of security, Logan Rafferty." He nodded toward the big man.

"Yes, I actually spoke to Mr. Rafferty when he

placed the nine-one-one call. The dispatcher transferred his call to me."

I suspected that Hannibal had a fairly small police department. That was probably why the 911 dispatcher had contacted Detective Travis first, rather than sending out some uniformed officers to the scene and letting them call in the detective, as it would have been done in a bigger city.

Williams introduced the other crew members who were there, then said, "And this is Ms. Delilah Dickinson."

Travis looked curiously at me. "Do you work on the riverboat, too, Ms. Dickinson?"

"No, I'm a travel agent," I told her. "Mr. Webster booked his cruise through my agency, and I'm leading the tour."

"Then what are you doing here?" the detective asked me with a frown. "Did you discover the body?"

"No, that was Henry here," Williams said.

Travis shook her head. "There are too many people here." She turned to the uniformed officers who'd accompanied her. "Take everybody except the captain and the man who discovered the body and hold them somewhere else for the time being, until I send for them."

"Wait just a minute," Rafferty protested. "I'm the head of security. I ought to be here."

"You will be when I'm ready to talk to you," Travis said. "Until then, maybe your office would be a good place for you and the rest of these people to wait."

Rafferty didn't like it, but after a second he gave a surly shrug. The cops shepherded us back along the corridor and up two sets of stairs to the deck where the security office was located.

As we went through the room where the video monitors were located, I asked Rafferty, "Are there any security cameras below decks?"

"You mean in the corridor where that storage closet is?" He shook his head. "Most of our video coverage is of the casino."

That came as no surprise. The casino was where the money was, after all.

"You've got to have some cameras out on deck, though," I said.

He grunted. "You ask too many questions."

As much as I hated to admit it, he was right. I was curious about what happened to Ben Webster, of course, and it bothered me that somebody had killed one of my clients. I thought that was a natural enough reaction. But it wasn't my job to find the killer, I reminded myself again.

Still, I glanced at the monitors as the cops took us through to Rafferty's office, just to get an idea of which areas on the boat the cameras covered.

The office was crowded with six people in it, especially when one of them was Rafferty. The cops told us to sit down and wait, but there weren't that many chairs. I didn't feel much like sitting, anyway, so I wound up crossing my arms and pacing back and forth. I couldn't even do that well, since there wasn't much room to pace.

Rafferty looked at me from behind his desk and said, "You don't think I had anything to do with that kid getting killed, do you?"

Before I could answer—and I wasn't sure what I would have said, anyway—one of the cops held up a finger and said, "No talking about the case. Detective Travis wouldn't like that."

Rafferty snorted. "What, you think we have to get our stories straight or something?"

"I can tell you this much," I said to the cop. "Mr. Rafferty and I aren't likely to be conspiring together on anything."

"The feeling is mutual," Rafferty said. He didn't have to add that the feeling was dislike.

The two stewards, if that's what they were, just looked uncomfortable. I'm not normally a hostile person, but something about Logan Rafferty brought out the worst in me, I guess.

We waited in silence for a while after that. It got on my nerves, and it must have bothered Rafferty, too. He grinned at the uniformed officers and said, "That Detective Travis is sort of hot, isn't she, boys?"

One of the cops cleared his throat and looked away. The other one just stonily ignored Rafferty. That seemed like a pretty good policy to me.

Finally the radio attached to one cop's belt squawked. He answered the call, and I heard Travis order, "Bring Mr. Rafferty down here."

The cop actually said, "Ten-four," and hung his radio back on its belt clip. He nodded to Rafferty and jerked a thumb toward the door. "Let's go."

That left the other cop watching me and the two stewards. It was a good thing we weren't desperate criminals, I thought.

Rafferty was gone for a long time. I was getting bored, and worse, I was hungry. Those appetizers I'd grabbed in the dining room hadn't lasted long. I guess seeing a dead body and fainting had burned off all the champagne, too. If I felt light-headed now, it was from being famished. I've always had a healthy appetite. Most petite Southern ladies do, once you get to know them.

I didn't expect to get anything to eat anytime soon, though. The murder investigation was more important than a growling stomach. I worried that Detective Travis would want to question the two stewards before she got around to me, and that it would be the middle of the night or later before she was done with me.

But when the cop brought Rafferty back to the office, he pointed at me and said, "You're next, ma'am. If you'll come with me . . . ?"

I didn't even try to ask him any questions on our way below decks. I knew he wouldn't answer them.

I was sort of hoping that Ben Webster's body had been taken away by now, but when we reached the corridor I saw that it was still stuffed into the storage closet. Crime scene technicians in Missouri State Police uniforms were photographing it and scouring the area around the door for evidence. Travis had moved back well away from the scene. Captain Williams was gone. I supposed that Travis had finished questioning him and told him to go back to running the boat. Not that there was probably much that needed to be done while we were docked, I thought.

"Ms. Dickinson," Travis began, "you're the owner and operator of Dickinson Literary Tours?" She had an open notebook in her hand, but she didn't consult it before asking me the question.

"That's right. I have a couple of employees, but it's my agency."

"Are either of those employees here on the *Southern Belle?*"

I shook my head. "No, they're back at the office in Atlanta. Well, they're not there right now, you understand, since it's, what, nearly midnight?"

She didn't directly respond to that, just said, "So you're handling this tour by yourself?"

"That's right. It's a relatively small tour, only about forty clients, and the arrangements were simple. There's really not that much that can go—"

I stopped, and for a second I thought Detective Travis might smile. But she didn't. She said, "You were about to say there's not much that can go wrong, weren't you?"

"Yeah." I shook my head and tried not to look toward the little closet where Ben Webster's body was. "Boy, I was wrong about that, wasn't I?"

"Tell me about Mr. Webster. Did you know him before he signed up to come on this tour?"

"No. I never even talked to him before lunch

today, back in St. Louis. He booked the trip using our Web page."

"You have all his information, I suppose? Credit card number, address, phone, all that?"

I nodded. "It's on my computer. Well, his credit card info isn't. It's on the office computer. But I can network with it and get the info if you want."

"Maybe later. Isn't it sort of unusual for a young man like Mr. Webster to be traveling alone, especially on a literary tour like this one?"

"Not really. I get clients like that pretty often. Anyway, the Mark Twain angle isn't the only draw on the boat. I'm sure a lot of people just come for the gambling."

"Oh, yes," Travis said. "The gambling. Any trouble there?"

I took a deep breath. I didn't have any reason to withhold the truth from her. And for all I knew, both Rafferty and Captain Williams had already told her all about it. If I didn't mention the incident that had occurred that afternoon, Travis was bound to wonder why.

Of course, if Williams and Rafferty *hadn't* said anything about what happened, then Travis might be suspicious of them once I brought it up.

But that was their lookout, not mine, so I said, "Yes, as a matter of fact, there *was* some trouble," and proceeded to tell her about it in as much detail as I could remember.

I couldn't read her face, couldn't tell if this was the first time she had heard the story or the third. She made some notes as I talked. When I was finished she asked, "Do you know the name of the man at the roulette wheel whom Mr. Webster accused of cheating?"

I shook my head. "No, I'm afraid not. But I'm sure the captain or Mr. Rafferty can tell you." *If they haven't already,* I thought.

"So after the meeting in Mr. Rafferty's office, you escorted Mr. Webster back to his cabin?"

Now I had to make up my mind. I didn't want to keep the truth from the police, even if it made me look a little foolish, so I said, "Not exactly."

For the first time, I saw a spark of real interest in Travis's eyes. "What do you mean by that?"

"I mean the rascal pulled a trick on me." I felt bad about calling him a rascal as soon as I said it, so I hurried on, "I mean, Mr. Webster led me to believe that the cabin he went to was the one assigned to him, but it really wasn't."

"All right, that's not clear to me. He went into someone else's cabin?"

"No," I said. "He stopped outside the door of Cabin Seventeen and *told* me it was his cabin, but he didn't go in just then, and I didn't wait to watch him go in. I left him there, just outside the door."

"How do you know it wasn't his cabin?"

"Because I went back there later looking for him, and I ran into the man who really has the cabin."

"What's his name?"

I hated to get Vince Mallory mixed up in this, but I didn't see that I had any choice. Besides,

Detective Travis could get the information in a matter of minutes by asking the captain or Rafferty.

"Vince Mallory," I said.

"Is he one of your clients as well?"

"Yes, he booked the tour through my agency."

"Were you acquainted with him before the cruise?"

"Nope. I mean, no."

"Another man traveling alone?"

"Yes, but in this case, I know why. He's a history and literature buff. Most of the clients who go on my tours are. In this case, Mr. Mallory is very interested in Mark Twain. He's going to write his doctoral dissertation on Twain."

At least, he was if he decided to go back to grad school, I thought. It seemed like a reasonable enough assumption.

Detective Travis said, "Do you have any idea why Mr. Webster would pretend that was his cabin when it really wasn't?"

"No. The only thing I can figure out was that he did it so I wouldn't be able to find him when I came looking for him."

"Why would he think you'd be looking for him later?"

"Well . . . he wouldn't. Unless he was already planning not to get off the boat when it docked at Hannibal."

That was pure speculation on my part, of course, but Detective Travis didn't seem bothered by it. She wrote some more in her notebook, then said, "You think he wasn't really going to take the deal Mr. Rafferty offered him.

He planned to cause some sort of trouble instead."

Those weren't actually questions, but I said, "That's what it looks like."

"But he didn't confide his plans to you."

I shook my head with some emphasis this time. "No, ma'am, he did not. If he had, I would've stayed right with him, grabbed him by the ear, and dragged him off the boat when we got here."

I would've done it, too.

Again I thought for a second that Detective Travis was going to smile. Instead she said, "You didn't see him after that?"

"No, ma'am. I looked for him when I saw he didn't get off the boat with the rest of the passengers, but I never found him."

"Where did you look?"

"All the areas on all three decks where passengers are allowed. I knocked on the door of his actual cabin, because I'd gotten the number of it from the passenger manifest that was e-mailed to me."

"Which cabin is that?"

I gave her the number. She made a note of it, then asked, "Did you try the door of that cabin to see if it was unlocked?"

"Uh, yeah, I did," I admitted. "But I knocked first and called out to him. He didn't answer. I didn't figure the door would be unlocked, but I tried the knob anyway."

And my fingerprints were all over that knob, I thought, as well as numerous other places in the cabin. It's a good thing I wasn't a professional criminal. I don't reckon I'd last a week.

I sort of hoped that Travis wouldn't follow up on that response, but naturally, she did. "Was the door unlocked?"

"It was."

"Did you go inside?"

"I called out to him, like I said, and when I opened the door and did it again and he still didn't answer . . . yeah, I went inside and took a look around. Right then, I was just concerned about him gettin' off the boat like he'd told Mr. Rafferty that he would."

"Did you see anything unusual, any signs of a struggle, anything like that?"

"No. His bags were gone. The cabin really looked like he'd come in, packed up, and left. That's what I thought had happened. I figured I must've just missed him leaving the boat somehow. I even walked into Hannibal to see if I could find where he'd rented a car to drive back down to St. Louis."

She looked at me, and again I couldn't read a blasted thing on her face. "You were taking a lot of interest in this young man's whereabouts."

"Well, sure I was," I said without hesitation. "I can tell this tour's gonna be popular with my clients. I didn't want any of them causin' so much trouble for the folks who run the boat that they'd ban Dickinson Literary Tours from future tours."

I didn't see how anybody could argue with the logic of that. Detective Travis nodded like she understood. "Is there anything else you can tell me about Mr. Webster or the things that happened earlier today?"

I thought about it and then shook my head. "I can't think of a thing."

"You don't know of anyone who'd want to hurt him?"

"No."

"What about the man he tried to punch in the casino?"

"From what I understand, he didn't even land that punch. Seems pretty far-fetched to me that anybody would break his neck hours later over it."

I didn't mention my theory that Webster might've been trying to sabotage the riverboat and Rafferty had caught him in the act. Travis would come up with that on her own, if she was any sort of detective.

"All right, Ms. Dickinson, thank you. That'll be all for now."

"For now?" I repeated.

For the first time, she actually smiled. "Until we have a better handle on this case, you won't be leaving the *Southern Belle*, Ms. Dickinson, and neither will anyone else. This riverboat is staying right where it is until I know who killed Ben Webster."

CHAPTER 8

I was tempted to argue with her. I had a business to run, and I was sure my clients all had lives they needed to get back to, not to mention all the other passengers on the boat.

But I didn't figure it would do any good, and anyway, plenty of other folks would be yelling once they found out they were stuck here while a murder investigation went on. I was sure once people started calling their lawyers, the situation would be resolved pretty quickly.

Detective Travis just wanted to keep the lid clamped down tight for as long as she could, and I couldn't blame her for that. Maybe it wouldn't take her long to discover who the killer was. Maybe he'd left his fingerprints on the storage closet door, or something like that.

Maybe pigs could fly, too, but I wasn't counting on it.

Since Travis was done with me, I asked, "Do I have to go back up to Rafferty's office?"

She shook her head. "No, I don't think that's

necessary. You can go where you want as long as you don't leave the boat." Her voice hardened. "I have an officer posted on the dock to make sure no one leaves. You're not planning on jumping overboard and trying to swim ashore, are you, Ms. Dickinson?"

"Not hardly," I said. "Huck and Jim might've jumped off that raft of theirs and swam around in the Mississippi, but it's not as clean now as it was back then. I'm not much of a swimmer, anyway."

"Do you have a cell phone?"

"Sure."

"Give me the number," she said, "in case I need to talk to you again."

Interrogate me again, that was what she meant, I thought. She copied down the number of my phone in her notebook and then turned the page. I took that to mean I was dismissed.

The uniformed cop who'd fetched me from Rafferty's office went as far as the main deck with me, then headed on up to the second deck. He was going to get one of the stewards, I thought. Detective Travis would be questioning both of them, even though they hadn't found the body. Captain Williams had just brought them below decks with him after he got the call from Henry about finding Ben Webster's corpse. But I supposed one of them might have noticed something that no one else had. It was possible, anyway.

I started to go to my cabin, then decided against it. Even though it was late, I was too upset by everything that had happened to just go to sleep. Besides, I was still hungry. I wondered if I could find anything to eat in the salon.

When I went in, the first person I saw was Vince Mallory. He sat on one of the divans sipping a drink and leafing through one of the books about Mark Twain that lay on a table in front of the divan. He looked up at me and smiled. He didn't look or act like he had heard anything about the murder. Neither did any of the other passengers in the salon, all of whom seemed to be having a good time.

I might have gone over and talked to Vince, but then I spotted Mark Lansing at the bar. He wasn't wearing his Mark Twain getup anymore, and I'm not sure any of the passengers other than me knew who he was. I smiled and waved at Vince, then headed for the bar to talk to Mark. Vince seemed like a pretty nice young man, but he was young enough to be, well, my son-in-law.

Anyway, Mark knew there had been some sort of problem earlier, and I was sure he was curious.

As I walked over to him, he stood up from the stool where he'd been sitting. "Are you all right, Delilah?" he asked.

"Yeah, I'm fine. A little tired and upset, maybe, but more hungry than anything else."

He shook his head. "There are some peanuts here on the bar, but I'm afraid that's all I can offer you."

"I'll take 'em." We sat down side by side, and he pushed the silver tray of peanuts over to me. I'd never thought that bar peanuts were particularly sanitary, but right then I didn't care. I picked up a handful and forced myself to eat them slowly.

"What happened?" Mark asked. "Why did the captain want to see you?"

I wasn't sure how much I ought to tell him. Detective Travis probably wanted the facts of the murder kept quiet while she was conducting her investigation. On the other hand, the rumor that somebody had been killed would be all over the boat by morning. I was sort of surprised that it wasn't already.

As I hesitated, Mark went on, "This has something to do with the police coming on the boat a little while ago, doesn't it?"

"You know about the police being here?"

"The word went around the crew pretty quickly," he said with a nod. "You can't keep trouble quiet."

That was true enough. So I said, "One of the passengers was killed."

Mark's eyes widened in surprise. "Really?" he said, then shook his head and went on, "Sorry. Of course you wouldn't kid about something like that. Do you know what happened? Was it an accident?"

"The police are looking into that now." That was sort of skimming past giving him a truthful answer, but it wasn't an outright lie, either. "Captain Williams notified me because it was one of my clients."

"Who?"

"Ben Webster."

I didn't see any sign of recognition in Mark's

eyes when I told him the name. There was no reason for him to know who Ben Webster was. I hadn't told him about the run-in Webster had had in the casino that afternoon.

"That's terrible," Mark said, slowly shaking his head. "You say the police are investigating?"

"That's right."

"The Hannibal PD?"

"That's right. A detective named Travis. And they have people from the State Police there, too."

Mark nodded. "Crime scene techs, more than likely. Small-town departments usually aren't equipped to handle murder investigations without some outside help."

"I didn't say it was murder," I pointed out.

"No, but the possibility must exist. The local cops wouldn't have called in the State Police if it was an obvious case of accidental death or suicide."

I narrowed my eyes at him. "For an actor, you seem to know a lot about police investigations."

"I used to be a lawyer, remember?"

I did recall that, now that he mentioned it. "Criminal law?"

"Some people say all lawyers are criminals," he replied with a grin. "But yeah, the firm I worked for handled a lot of criminal cases."

"So you were a defense attorney."

He shrugged. I could understand why he didn't want to come right out and admit it. A lot of people didn't like defense attorneys. Me, I just wished society didn't have any need for them. Divorce lawyers, too.

But I didn't want to start brooding about that. Anyway, I was pretty much over my divorce, and there were plenty of other things going on to occupy my attention. So I pushed those thoughts out of my mind and said, "Well, I don't care what you used to do. Now you're Mark Twain."

"That's right. And Twain said everyone is a moon and has a dark side that he never shows to anybody."

I wasn't sure what he meant by that, so I ate some more peanuts. "Is there anywhere on this boat a person can get an actual meal at this time of night?"

"I suppose we could raid the galley. I'd invite you back to my cabin for a late supper, but we just met, and besides, I don't have any food there anyway."

I was sort of glad he didn't invite me to his cabin. I wasn't sure what my answer would have been. There was a 99 percent chance I would have declined, but I didn't quite trust that other 1 percent.

Somebody came up to the bar on my other side. I looked around to see Vince Mallory motioning to the bartender for a refill on his drink. He smiled at me and asked, "Did you ever find that fellow you were looking for earlier, Ms. Dickinson?"

"Yeah, I saw him a while ago." I didn't say that I'd talked to Ben Webster.

Nobody would ever do that again. Even if they did, Webster wouldn't hear them.

"Get everything straightened out?"

I thought about the way Webster's arms and legs had been bent so that the killer could force him into that cramped space and I made an effort not to shudder. "No, but, uh, I'm sure it will be in time."

"I hope so." He picked up his fresh drink. "Have a good evening."

It was too late for that, I thought as he walked back to the divan. Especially if I wasn't going to Mark Lansing's cabin.

"How about that raid on the galley?" Mark asked when Vince was gone.

I nodded. "Let's do it," I said.

The kitchen—or galley, as I guess it was properly called, since we were on a boat—was deserted at this time of night. The cooks would be there early the next morning to start preparing breakfast, but that was still several hours away.

"You're not gonna get in trouble for this, are you?" I asked Mark as he rummaged through the big refrigerators and the pantry.

"Not if nobody knows who did it," he answered with a grin.

"Now, dadgum it, I'm serious. I don't want you gettin' fired or anything just because I missed my supper."

"Don't worry, nothing's going to happen to me. How does bacon and toast and scrambled eggs sound to you? I know that's the sort of thing people eat for breakfast—"

I checked my watch. "It's after midnight. Close enough for government work."

He fired up the grill and got busy. "When we're finished I can clean everything up so that nobody will even know we were here."

"Let me guess. Before you were a lawyer-turned-actor, you were a short-order cook in a diner."

"Actually, I did work in a diner when I was in college. Mostly as a busboy, though. But I got on the grill a few times. Anyway, whipping up a nice, greasy batch of bacon and eggs is like riding a bicycle. You never forget how."

"That sounds delicious." I opened one of the refrigerators. "Is there any orange juice in here? If we're gonna have breakfast for our late-night snack, we might as well go all the way."

I found the juice and poured it into glasses and wondered why I'd used a loaded expression like "go all the way." At least, it was loaded for people of a certain age. I was darned if I was going to call it "hooking up," like my teenage nieces would. But I shouldn't be thinking about such things, even in the back of my mind, I told myself. Even if Will Burke and I weren't what you'd call exclusive. Even if—and this was probably the best reason—I hadn't been looking at the body of a murder victim an hour earlier, which, in fact, I had.

I realized I was on the verge of overthinking things. A common failing of mine. So I shoved all of it out of my head and concentrated instead on how appetizing the bacon smelled as it fried and how tart and good the orange juice was as I drank some of it. I told myself to just live in the moment for now.

Seeing what had happened to Ben Webster was a good enough motive for doing that.

Mark had the food ready in a few minutes. We ate standing up at one of the counters, wolfing bacon, scrambled eggs, and toast and washing it down with the cold juice, and it was a fine meal, let me tell you.

"You have any Mark Twain quotes about food?" I asked.

"Not right offhand, but let me think about it for a while and I'll see what I can come up with."

"You must have memorized everything Sam Clemens ever wrote."

He laughed. "No, but I've watched the DVD of *Mark Twain Tonight!* with Hal Holbrook so many times the disc is wearing out, I think. My performance is an homage to his."

"Homage bein' French for blatant copy, right?"

That brought an even bigger laugh from him. "Right. How can you impersonate Mark Twain and *not* swipe from Holbrook? He's the gold standard."

"I don't know. I think you bring your own slant to the role. You might be even better at portraying Twain as a young man than as the doddering old-timer that everybody else portrays."

He frowned and rubbed his jaw. "Now there's an interesting thought. Instead of doing Twain as an old man remembering his youth as a river pilot, I could portray him when he actually *was* a pilot." I heard the excitement come into Mark's voice. "That's a really good idea. Thanks, Delilah."

What he did next was just expressing that gratitude, I told myself.

He leaned over and kissed me.

CHAPTER 9

He tasted like bacon and orange juice and the champagne we'd had earlier. His hand closed on the bare flesh of my upper arm, below the sleeve of my dress. His grip was gentle, but strong enough to be warm and firm. My arms wanted to lift up and go around his neck.

I stopped them. Because, unlike what I had told him about playing Mark Twain as a younger man, what we were doing now was *not* a good idea.

Mark must have sensed the tension that sprang up in me, because he let go of my arm and pulled his head back. "Sorry," he murmured. "I don't know what came over me. I know we just met earlier today—"

"No, it's all right," I told him. I didn't want him beating himself up over something as nice as that kiss had been. "I'm just tired, that's all, and upset about what happened to Mr. Webster."

"Of course you are. I'm an idiot."

"Not hardly. I enjoyed it. Maybe your timing

could've been a mite better, that's all. How about a rain check?"

He grinned in relief. "Sure. That's better than a slap in the face any day."

We went back to talking about Mark Twain and finished up the food. I'd be lying if I said the kiss wasn't lingering in the back of my mind, though.

I liked Mark Lansing. Maybe liked him too much under the circumstances. I had a business to run in Atlanta, and he had his job on the riverboat cruising between St. Louis and Hannibal. If we tried to date, we wouldn't be able to see each other very often, and I've never been much of a believer in long-distance relationships. I didn't have *that* good a track record with short-distance relationships.

So I told myself that maybe it would be better to just accept what had happened between us this evening for what it was—a pleasant flirtation and a darn nice kiss—and move on. That would sure simplify things.

When we were finished with the meal, I helped Mark clean up. His prediction turned out to be true. Unless one of the cooks noticed that some of the bacon, eggs, bread, and orange juice were gone, nobody would know that we had been here.

"I'll walk you back to your cabin," Mark offered.

"That's very gentlemanly of you," I said, "but not necessary."

He frowned. "One person has already been killed on this riverboat, and there might be a murderer running around loose. I'm not going to let you walk all the way back to your cabin by yourself."

That was a good point, and Mark didn't even know for sure yet that Ben Webster had been murdered. I did. Even though I couldn't think of any reason the killer would want to come after me next, I didn't see any point in taking chances.

And it was possible, I realized, that if the murderer knew about my connection with Webster, he might worry that the young man had told me something I shouldn't know, something that the cops might use to get on his trail. In that case, he might decide that the easiest thing to do would be to get rid of me.

That made a shiver go through me. Mark saw it and asked, "Are you cold?"

It was a warm night. I shook my head and said, "No, I'm fine. I could just use some sleep, that's all."

He linked his arm with mine. "Sure, it's getting really late. Come on."

We left the kitchen. Galley, I mean. Mark knew his way around the boat and took me through some corridors where passengers weren't allowed to get us back out on the main deck. The lights had been lowered for the night in most places except the casino. Just like in Vegas, it stayed open around the clock while the *Southern Belle* was on a cruise.

As we walked along, I looked for security cameras and spotted one or two, tucked away in unobtrusive corners. In my inexpert opinion, though, there was a lot of deck area the cameras didn't cover. As Logan Rafferty had said, the main concern of the security personnel was the casino.

I was sure Detective Travis would study whatever surveillance footage was available to her, anyway. But I didn't hold out much hope that she'd find pictures of the killer dragging Ben Webster's body below decks. I had a hunch the killer was pretty familiar with the riverboat and knew how to avoid the cameras.

When we stopped in front of the door to my cabin, I said, "Thank you for the parts of the evening that were lovely."

"And the less said about the unlovely parts, the better?" Mark asked.

I thought about Ben Webster's dead face and said, "Yeah. Definitely."

He leaned toward me and brushed his lips over mine. No passion this time, just a friendly gesture. "Good night."

"Night," I said.

He squeezed my shoulder for a second and backed off a step. I realized he was waiting for me to open the door and go inside. Maybe he wanted to make sure I hadn't brought him to a cabin belonging to someone else, like Ben Webster had done with me. Maybe he just wanted to know that I had gotten inside safely before he left. I took my key out of my purse, slid it into the lock, and turned it. I opened the door and reached inside to flip on the light.

Then I stepped back with a surprised gasp.

Mark was beside me instantly. "What's wrong?"

I pointed through the open door without saying anything.

"Son of a *bitch*!" Mark said as he looked at the mess inside the cabin. Someone had searched it, and he hadn't been too careful about it, either. He had torn off the bedclothes, pulled everything out of the closet and the tiny chest of drawers, and upended my bags, dumping their contents on the now-bare mattress.

I started through the door, but Mark grabbed my arm and hung on, urging me back away from the opening. "You can't go in there," he said. "Whoever did it might still be inside."

"No, he's not," I said. "You can see the whole cabin from the door."

"Not the bathroom."

He had a point there. The bathroom door wasn't closed, but it was pulled up so that there was only a small gap. That was how I'd left it— but that didn't mean someone couldn't be hiding in there. The intruder could have pushed the door almost closed again from the other side.

My laptop had been in its case inside the closet. That was the only really valuable thing I had with me. I didn't see the case anywhere inside the room. It might be on the other side of the bed, out of sight from where I was, I thought. I wanted to know if it was gone.

"Was the door locked when you opened it just now?" Mark asked. He still had hold of my arm with his left hand.

"Yeah, I think so," I told him. "That doesn't really mean anything, though. You can just turn the little button on the knob and lock the door when you go out."

He nodded. That must have been what the intruder had done. I was willing to bet there were no fingerprints on the knob, though. The thief would have had sense enough to wear gloves.

That's all I thought it was, a simple burglary. Sure, the place was torn up like someone had searched it thoroughly, I thought as my speeding pulse started to slow down and reason reasserted itself in my brain. But it was much more likely that someone had broken in to look for valuables. That would explain the search, too. There was no reason in the world this incident had to be connected with Ben Webster's murder.

But that was the first place my brain went, anyway. The killer was after me, too. He thought I had some sort of evidence that would convict him, and he had broken into my cabin to look for it.

When I thought about all the wandering around on the boat by myself I had done earlier in the day, not to mention in Hannibal, I got a cold, scared feeling in the pit of my stomach. The murderer could have been stalking me then. It might just be luck I was still alive.

I gave myself a stern warning not to overreact. I said, "I guess we'd better report this."

"To the police, or to Logan Rafferty?"

I glanced at the dock. A couple of police cars were still parked there, although the crime scene SUV with the State Police emblem on it that had been there earlier was gone. I supposed the technicians had done their work and left. Detective Travis might still be on board the riverboat, though.

And to tell the truth, I didn't want to have anything more to do with Logan Rafferty than I had to.

"Let's go see if we can find the cops," I said. I reached out, hooked the doorknob with one finger, and pulled the door closed.

Mark shook his head. "Call them instead. We should stay here, in case the guy's still in the cabin and tries to sneak out."

"So we can confront him?" I shook my head. "I don't think that's a very good idea."

"You're probably right," Mark admitted. "Let's move down there to the other end of the deck so we can keep an eye on the door. That way if he tries to get out, at least we'll see him."

I wasn't convinced at all that the burglar was still in the cabin, but I couldn't rule it out. So we did what Mark suggested, walking quickly down to the other end of the deck and glancing over our shoulders with just about every step. When we had put enough distance between us and the cabin to be safe, I got out my cell phone and called 911.

"Is Detective Travis still on the *Southern Belle* riverboat?" I asked when the dispatcher answered.

He didn't answer my question, instead asked one of his own. "What's your emergency, ma'am?"

That was standard procedure. I said, "There's been a burglary on the riverboat *Southern Belle*, docked here at the foot of Center Street." I gave him the cabin number. "My name is Delilah Dickinson. I spoke to Detective Travis earlier tonight about another matter, and I thought if she was still on board, she might like to see this."

"Is the perpetrator still in the cabin?"

"I don't know. I don't think so, but I'm not sure."

"Is anyone hurt? Were you assaulted?"

"No to both of those questions. Whoever it was, he got into the cabin while nobody was there."

"You're certain you've been burglarized?"

"Pretty sure. I think my laptop is gone." I was getting pretty impatient. "Are you going to send somebody or not?" I didn't even care that much anymore if it was Travis.

"Yes, ma'am, I've already text-messaged Detective Travis. She should be on her way."

The wonders of modern technology. "Thank you," I said.

"Would you like to stay on the line with me until the detective gets there?"

Just then I saw Travis emerge from one of the stairways that led between decks. I said, "That's not necessary, thanks. Here she comes now," and folded up the phone, breaking the connection.

"Ms. Dickinson," Travis said as she came up to me. I couldn't tell if she was annoyed or not. As usual, she didn't allow much emotion to appear on her face. She looked vaguely curious, though, as she glanced at Mark.

"This is Mark Lansing," I told her. "He works

here on the riverboat." I didn't explain that he did a performance in the salon as Mark Twain. That didn't seem to have anything to do with what was going on here.

I halfway expected Travis to pull out her notebook and write down Mark's name, but she didn't. Instead she said, "You reported that someone broke into your cabin?"

"That's right." I pointed. "It's over there."

"The burglar's not still inside?"

"I don't think so."

Travis reached into the blazer she wore—just like a travel agent's or a Realtor's, I realized— and brought out a gun. It was a small-caliber semiautomatic, probably a 9mm. I didn't know enough about guns to recognize the make.

"Stay here," she said. "I'll check it out."

"Shouldn't you have some backup?" Mark asked.

"I'm fine." She sounded a little irritated.

"Let me come with you," Mark suggested.

"Just stay here," Travis snapped. She started toward my cabin, glancing back at me to ask, "Is the door unlocked?"

"Yeah, it is."

She nodded and moved closer to the door, using her left hand to grip the wrist of her right hand, which held the gun. Just like they do on TV, in other words.

When she reached the door, she used her left hand to twist the knob. Then she pushed the door open with her foot and went in fast, turning from side to side so that she could sweep the gun back and forth. I realized that I was holding my breath, waiting for shots to sound inside the room, but there weren't any. Travis moved farther into the cabin, so Mark and I couldn't see her from where we were, but she wasn't gone long. When she stepped out again a minute or so later, she held the gun down alongside her leg.

"You can come in," she called to us. "The cabin's empty."

That didn't really surprise me. We hurried along the deck and went into the cabin. Travis said, "Look around and see if you can tell what's missing, if anything."

Something was missing, I was certain of that, and sure enough, my laptop was gone. It took me only a couple of minutes to look everywhere in the cabin it could have been. Somebody had grabbed it, case and all, and taken it out of there.

"Anything else?" Travis asked when I told her about the computer.

"I didn't have anything else really valuable," I said as I pawed through the mess. "I'm wearing the only jewelry that means anything to me, at least that I brought along on this trip. My money and my phone are in my purse."

I looked around as best I could, just to be sure, then reported, "Nope, the only thing that seems to be gone is the laptop."

"Describe it."

"It's a laptop computer," I said, trying not to sound exasperated.

"Make, model, serial number?"

"I don't know." I knew the brand, and which

operating system it ran, but that was about all. "That information will be on file in my office records, though. I can get it. I'll just send an e-mail—" I stopped and took a deep breath. "Or not. I can call the office in the morning and get the information."

"You'll need to do that," Travis said with a nod. "You should let us know so we can add the information to the report. You'll need that for your insurance company when you file a claim for the computer."

"You don't think there's a chance you'll be able to find it?"

She slipped the gun back into the holster clipped to her belt. "There's always a chance, but I wouldn't count on it. I'm sorry, but we have other cases that are more pressing."

"Like findin' out who killed Ben Webster?"

Travis frowned. She didn't like me bringing that up in front of Mark, I guess. And as soon as the words were out of my mouth, I realized that I had just confirmed for him that Webster was murdered, when earlier I had been deliberately vague about it. It was too late to take it back now, though.

"We'll be in touch," Travis said. She nodded to both of us and walked out of the cabin, leaving me and Mark there.

"So," he said as he looked at me, "your client was murdered, eh?"

CHAPTER 10

I met Mark's eyes squarely with mine. I'm no shrinking violet. If he wanted to get mad at me because I hadn't told him the full truth, then he could go right ahead and be mad.

"That's right," I said. "I don't reckon the detective would want me to say anything else, but since the cat's already out of the bag about that part, I'm not gonna deny it."

"You could explain why you didn't just tell me to start with."

"Like I said, I didn't think Detective Travis would want me runnin' around all over the boat tellin' folks that there'd been a murder."

"People are going to find out anyway."

"Yeah, but I didn't want to be to blame for it."

He thought about it for a moment, then started to nod. "Yeah, I suppose that makes sense. It wasn't that you didn't trust me in particular."

"Shoot, no! I reckon I trust you more than anybody else on this boat."

I wasn't sure what made me say that, or even

why I felt that way. But it was true. I trusted Mark Lansing. Maybe it was because the first time I'd met him, he looked just like Mark Twain. Who wouldn't trust Mark Twain?

He gestured toward my cabin. "Where are you going to stay tonight? That's a crime scene."

"Not much of one, the way Detective Travis was acting. She didn't tell me I couldn't stay there."

"Everything's torn up."

"Not really. I can put it back in order pretty quick, I imagine." I wasn't going to be too happy about spending the night in there alone, knowing that somebody had already broken in once and could do it again, but I sure as heck wasn't going to ask Mark to stay with me, even though a part of me sort of liked the idea.

"Look, let's go see the captain. Surely he can find you another cabin."

I shook my head. "From what I've heard, the boat's fully booked. There aren't any empty cabins."

"Then you're going to stay in my cabin," Mark declared. "Nobody would think to look for you there."

I gave him the skunk eye. "Savin' me from a return visit by a burglar, is that what you've got in mind, Mr. Lansing?"

"What? Wait a minute!" He started shaking his head. "You've got me all wrong, Delilah. You can have my cabin for the night. I'll stay up in the salon."

It was my turn to shake my head. "You can't do that. You wouldn't get a bit of sleep."

"Why do I need sleep? I don't have a performance again until the day after tomorrow. I'll be plenty rested by then. Anyway, have you seen those big armchairs in the salon? I'll prop my feet up and sleep just fine in one of them."

"Well . . ." It was a tempting offer, and I was convinced now that Mark didn't have any ulterior motives. Even though I had known him less than twelve hours, he seemed like an honorable fella to me.

"If you don't say yes, I'm going to have to sleep here on the deck, right outside your door, to protect you."

"I guess chivalry's not dead after all." I laughed. "All right. It's a sweet offer, and I'll take you up on it. Let's be careful, though. I don't want folks seein' me slippin' in and out of your cabin. If I'm gonna be bringin' tours on this boat on a regular basis, I don't want to get a bad reputation among the crew."

I threw a couple of things in a bag and then locked my cabin. I could straighten everything out the next morning. Mark and I went up onto the second deck where the crew had their quarters. I don't know if he was officially considered part of the crew or not, but his cabin was up there with the others.

By this time of night, nobody was moving around. The diehard gamblers were in the casino, the boozers were in the salon, and everybody else had returned from sightseeing and turned in for the night. Mark unhooked the slender chain across the deck that had a sign on it reading AUTHORIZED PERSONNEL ONLY and led me past it to the crew cabins. He unlocked his door, pushed it open, and held out an arm to usher me inside.

The cabin looked about the same as the ones used by the passengers. If anything, it was a little more spartan in its furnishings. But the bed was made, instead of stripped, and Mark's belongings hadn't been strewn all over the floor.

He took a phone out of his pocket and said, "Put my number in your phone, and if you have any problems during the night, don't hesitate to call me."

We engaged in the modern-day ritual of programming each other's numbers into our phones, and then I stifled a yawn and said, "Well, I guess this is good night."

"Yeah."

I hoped he wasn't going to linger until things got awkward. He didn't, thank goodness. He just smiled and went to the door, pausing there to say, "Be sure to lock this and put the chain on after I'm gone."

"I will," I promised.

He smiled again, lifted a hand in farewell, and was gone, closing the door quietly behind him. I felt a little bad about him having to spend the night in the salon. I hoped he actually would be able to get some sleep.

Once I'd made sure the door was locked and fastened the chain, I sat on the bed and sighed in a mixture of weariness and relief. This cruise hadn't gone like I'd planned so far, but it wasn't my fault that Ben Webster had gone and gotten himself murdered, or that somebody had broken into my cabin.

My fault or not, though, once news of the murder broke in the media, it wouldn't be good publicity for Dickinson Literary Tours. And chances were, some eager-beaver reporter would Google my name and find out that a couple of murders had taken place on one of my tours the year before, which would make my involvement in this one even more newsworthy. If it bleeds, it leads, as the old saying goes.

But there was nothing I could do about it tonight. Nothing I could do about it, period, except hope that the police found Ben Webster's killer quickly and that his death would wind up having nothing directly to do with my agency. That may sound a little callous, but Ben Webster was beyond caring about now. I had tried to help him, and that hadn't worked out. If he had just gone to his cabin and stayed there until the boat docked in Hannibal, then gotten off, like he was supposed to, he might still be alive. Instead, he had started roaming around the *Southern Belle* and had wound up dead.

But why? I asked myself. The only motive I'd considered was the idea that Logan Rafferty had killed him because Webster was trying to sabotage the boat some way. But I had no proof that any such thing had happened. Maybe Webster's murderer had followed him onto the boat for the express purpose of killing him. I didn't know anything about the young man's background. He could have all sorts of enemies who'd been stalking him.

That sounded too melodramatic to me, even as the thought went through my head. But one thing was certain: Ben Webster had had at least one enemy, and a bad one, at that.

Detective Travis would investigate his background, I told myself. She would find out if he had anything in his past that would make someone want him dead. That was her job, not mine, and I was glad of it.

I took off my blue dress, washed up, removed my make-up, and put on the pair of pajamas I had thrown into the bag I brought along. By the time I'd brushed my teeth, the late hour was catching up with me. I almost stumbled from sleepiness as I went to the bed, pulled back the covers, and crawled in. As I snapped off the lamp on the little table beside the bed, I figured I'd doze off as soon as my head hit the pillow.

Naturally, it didn't work out that way.

When I closed my eyes, my brain started filling up with all the things that had happened since I'd arrived in St. Louis that morning. I replayed the luncheon, boarding the boat, cruising up the Mississippi, and meeting Mark Lansing in his Mark Twain getup. It hadn't been long after that that things had started to go south, and I don't mean down the river.

Maybe I was searching my memory for clues without really being aware of it. I had figured out who had killed those folks on the plantation, after all. But despite that I didn't think of myself as a detective. I was just a small-business owner trying to minimize the damage to my business.

While I was lying there in the darkness, turning those things over in my head and wondering why the heck I couldn't just go to sleep, I heard a noise. It wasn't very loud, but it came from somewhere close by and my instincts told me that it shouldn't be there. After a second I realized what it was.

Somebody had just slipped a key into the doorknob.

Mark had a key; I knew that. Maybe he had forgotten something that he needed and thought he could slip in and get it without disturbing me.

But he had told me to be sure to fasten the chain on the door, I recalled. He would know that he couldn't get into the cabin without waking me.

Maybe he wanted to wake me. Maybe he had decided that he didn't want to spend the night in the salon after all.

Maybe I was about to have to make a decision I didn't really want to be forced to make.

Or maybe the killer had figured out where I was and had come back to finish his work.

That thought sent a chill through me. I didn't have anything to fight off an attacker other than some pepper spray in my purse, and I didn't recall seeing anything in the cabin that could be used as a weapon except maybe the lamp. And it wasn't big and heavy enough to be very effective as a club. Of course, I could scream—nothing wrong with my lungs, after all—and maybe somebody in a nearby cabin would come to help me.

That might be my best bet, I decided as I fought down a surge of panic.

But I didn't want to start hollering if the person who had just unlocked the door was Mark. That would be embarrassing. So I threw back the covers and swung my legs out of bed, then stood up as I heard the knob turn slowly and quietly.

My instincts told me to run, but there was nowhere to run to in the cabin. Instead I moved silently toward the doorway as it eased open. I was about to open my mouth to say *Mark?* when the chain stopped the door from opening any farther. A voice spoke in an urgent whisper.

"Mark? Mark, it's me. Let me in."

A *woman's* voice.

That stopped me in my tracks. Why would a woman have a key to Mark's cabin and expect the chain to be unfastened in the middle of the night, as if he were expecting her?

Well, there was one obvious answer, of course. He could have a girlfriend among the crew. He might even be involved with one of the passengers. He hadn't *said* anything to me about having a girlfriend, and he'd kissed me, after all. But let's face it—that wouldn't be the first time a fella kissed a woman other than the one he was supposed to be romantically linked with.

The damn dog.

As soon as that thought went through my head, I told myself to stop jumping to conclusions. Maybe there was a logical, reasonable explanation for this woman trying to sneak into Mark's room in the middle of the night that didn't have anything to do with hanky-panky. *Suuuure* there was.

But either way I wanted to know who she was. With her whispering like that, I hadn't been able to recognize her voice. So I leaned toward the door and asked in a whisper of my own, "Who's there?"

"*Oh!*"

The exclamation told me that Mark's late-night visitor was just as surprised to find another woman in his cabin as I had been when she unlocked the door. She didn't say anything else. She just jerked the door closed, and the rapid patter of footsteps on the dock told me that she was running away.

Consumed by curiosity, I hurried to the door and fumbled with the chain. I wasn't thinking about mysterious killers anymore. I wanted to get a look at the woman. When I finally got the chain unfastened, I threw the door open and stuck my head out.

I was just in time to see a flash of blond hair and the flutter of a robe as she ducked around the corner at the far end of the dimly lit deck. She was moving fast, and I didn't get a good look at all. For a second I thought about chasing after her, but then I realized how insane that was. Anybody who saw me running along the deck of a riverboat in my pajamas would think that I was a total loon, and they'd be right. Plus there was the whole lurking murderer business to consider.

I retreated into the cabin, closed the door, and fastened the chain again.

As frustrating and puzzling as this incident was, I knew there was one good way to find out what had just happened here. In the morning, when I saw Mark Lansing again, I would ask him why strange women were sneaking into his cabin well after midnight. Of course, I reminded myself, *I* was a strange woman myself, or at least I had been to Mark until about twelve hours earlier, and here I was in his cabin. In his bed, for that matter. But that was different.

Considering everything that had happened, it took a long time for me to get to sleep. *That* didn't surprise me at all.

CHAPTER 11

I had a restless what was left of the night and woke up early the next morning feeling almost as tired as when I'd gone to sleep. The gray light coming in around the edges of the curtain over the cabin's single window told me that it wasn't dawn yet. I didn't think I could sleep anymore, though, so I got out of bed.

Hoping that a shower might wake me up, I went into the bathroom and started the water running, then looked around. Mark's shaving kit sat on the tiny vanity, partially unzipped. I felt the urge to poke around in it a little, but I resisted. I wouldn't want him digging around in my purse or my make-up bag, so I had to honor his privacy, too.

When I had the water at the temperature I liked, I took off my pajamas and hung them on the hook on the back of the bathroom door, then stepped into the hot shower. It felt mighty good. I stayed there for what seemed like a long time, letting the hot water work out all the kinks in my body.

I wished it could do as good a job working out the mental kinks, but I knew that wasn't going to happen.

Finally, when the water began to run cool, I turned it off and pushed back the curtain to step out onto the little mat. I pulled an unused towel from the rack and started to dry. I had pushed the bathroom door up without closing it quite all the way, so most of the steam from the hot shower had been trapped. The mirror was completely fogged up and probably would be for a while, but the steamy bathroom felt good. I like a nice hot shower, even in the summer.

When I finished drying, I moved to hang up the towel. As I did, I bumped the shaving kit with my hip. There wasn't much room on the vanity to start with, since it was so small, and the leather kit was perched near the edge. When I bumped it, it slid off and fell to the floor.

It landed on the tile with a heavy *clunk.*

The sound brought a frown to my face. Just how heavy could a man's razor and toothbrush be, anyway? I bent over and picked up the shaving kit, set it on the vanity. It was heavy, all right.

Feeling a little guilty about what I was doing, I unzipped the top the rest of the way and looked inside.

The first thing I saw was a clear plastic bag with a tube of toothpaste and a toothbrush inside it. The toothbrush had one of those plastic covers over the bristles. Next to the bag was one of those razors with multiple blades. I don't know how many this one had, but it's only a matter of time until they come up with a twenty-two-blade razor that a guy has to move only an inch to shave his whole face. There was a can of shaving cream and a plastic bottle of aftershave, plus some first-aid stuff and a package of cotton swabs. Nothing out of the ordinary there, and although the shaving cream might have made the clunking noise when the bag hit the floor, I knew it hadn't.

No, the gun underneath all the other stuff was what had made the noise.

I saw the barrel and part of the cylinder poking out and recognized them for what they were, even though at the same time my brain was rebelling at the thought. Who carries a revolver in a shaving kit?

Well, Mark Lansing, for one, obviously. I had the testimony of my own eyes for that. I moved the stuff in the bag so I could get a better look at the gun.

It wasn't very big. A .32? A .38? I don't know. The whole thing wasn't over six inches long, and the barrel accounted for about two inches of that. The handle had plastic grips made to look like wood with a little checkered pattern in it. The finish on the rest of the gun was silvery. It looked sort of like a toy, but it was the real thing. The feeling of danger that came off it told me that.

And I had knocked it off onto the floor. Revolvers sometimes went off when they were dropped. Maybe it wasn't loaded. I didn't want to touch it, so I picked up one end of the bag and tilted it so I could look at the chambers in the cylinder from the back. As far as I could tell, they were empty. So at least the gun wasn't loaded.

That didn't take away from the fact that Mark had a gun in his shaving kit. And a package of condoms, too, I saw now, nestled next to the can of shaving cream. Obviously a man who wanted to be fully protected: Trojans *and* a Smith & Wesson.

I pushed that crazy thought away and set the bag back on the vanity. I pulled the zipper part of the way closed, like it had been when I found it. Then I realized I was standing there naked in the bathroom of a man who packed heat and had mysterious women visiting him in the middle of the night.

It was time to get out of Dodge.

The night before I had stuck a clean pair of slacks and a blouse in my bag, along with clean underwear, of course. I got dressed in a hurry, put on as little make-up as I could get by with, and ran a brush through my hair. I'm lucky that it doesn't take a lot of work.

As I came out of the bathroom I heard my phone ringing in my purse.

Mark was calling, I saw as I got the phone out and checked the display. I didn't know whether I wanted to talk to him or not. I had plenty of questions for him. Well, two big ones really: *Who was that woman? What's the deal with the gun?* But I thought it might be better to ask them in person.

If I ignored the call, though, he might get

worried and show up to pound on the door. I didn't want to draw any attention to the fact that I had spent the night in his cabin, so I opened the phone and said, "Hello?"

"Good morning," he said, sounding cheery as all get-out. "It's not too early, is it? I was afraid I might wake you."

"No, I was up," I said. I thought, *I've been up long enough to take a shower and find the gun in your shaving kit,* but I didn't say it.

"How about some breakfast?" Mark asked. "I realize it'll be our second breakfast today, but—"

"That's fine," I said.

"Should I come to the cabin and get you, or would you rather just meet in the dining room?"

"Let's meet in the dining room," I said. "I'll be there in ten minutes."

If my rather abrupt attitude puzzled him, his voice didn't show it. "Sounds good," he said, still cheery. "I'll see you there."

I broke the connection and looked at the phone for a second, then said, "You sure will, bucko."

Mark beat me to the dining room. He was sitting at one of the tables when I walked in. He smiled and raised a hand to catch my attention, but I had already seen him and started toward him.

He stood and held my chair for me as I sat down. I've been around long enough that such gestures don't bother me. As he sat down, he asked, "How did you sleep?"

"Fine," I said.

"The bed was comfortable enough?"

"Sure."

Tiny frown creases appeared on his forehead. "Is something wrong?"

"Wrong? No. What makes you ask?"

"I don't know, you just seem a little . . . different this morning."

I shrugged. "I don't feel any different."

Now that was a bald-faced lie. I felt a lot different than I had the night before. It bothered me that he hadn't told me the truth. Not all the truth, anyway. Maybe he hadn't actually lied, but he had left out a lot of stuff.

I wanted him to tell me on his own. I didn't like the idea of having to drag answers out of him. If he really was interested in me, as he'd acted, he owed it to me to be on the up-and-up. I hadn't been deceptive with him.

Other than not telling him up front that Ben Webster had been murdered, I reminded myself. I had sort of fudged the truth about that for a little while.

"If something's bothering you," he said, "you need to just tell me."

Of course he'd feel that way, I thought. He was a man. But if that's what he wanted . . .

I was about to open my mouth to ask him about the mysterious woman and the gun when someone paused beside me and a deep voice said, "Good morning, Ms. Dickinson."

I looked up to see Captain Williams standing there. He looked tired, as if he hadn't slept much the night before. I guessed that was prob-

ably true. I'd think that having a passenger murdered on board would bother most boat cap-
tains.

"Hello, Captain," I said. "Any news?"

I didn't have to specify what sort of news I was
asking about, I thought. It was pretty doggoned
obvious. My hope was that he'd tell me Detective Travis had found and arrested the killer and
that we'd be on our way back to St. Louis later in
the day, as scheduled.

Instead he shook his head and looked grim.
"I'm afraid not," he said. He glanced at Mark,
nodded, and added, "Mr. Lansing."

I could tell he was wondering just how well informed Mark was about what had happened, so
I said, "Mark knows about the—" I started to say
murder, then changed my mind. "Incident," I
said instead. I was sure that rumors would
spread throughout the boat, especially if we
didn't start back to St. Louis on schedule, but
for now most of the passengers probably didn't
know about the murder. No sense in starting a
panic until you had to, I thought.

Captain Williams put a hand on one of the
empty chairs at the table and asked, "Do you
mind?"

"Go right ahead," Mark told him, then
glanced at me. "That is, if it's all right with
Delilah."

"Sure. Sit down, Captain."

Williams pulled back the chair and sat down
with a sigh. "I've been up most of the night," he
said, keeping his voice pitched low so that the
early diners at the other tables wouldn't hear the

conversation over their own voices and the noises coming from the kitchen. "I thought it best to go ahead and notify Mr. Gallister's office about what happened. I wasn't expecting Mr. Gallister himself to call me and demand to know what's being done. I was on the phone with him for a long time. He's coming up here himself to make sure that the matter is resolved in a satisfactory manner."

That surprised me. I said, "I didn't figure a tycoon like Charles Gallister would have time for something like that."

"He's a very hands-on owner." The captain didn't look happy about that fact, either. "No detail is too small for his attention, he always says. And murder is no small detail."

I couldn't argue with that.

"Has that detective found out anything yet?" I asked.

"If she has, she hasn't shared it with me. She was on board most of the night, I think."

"Does she still plan to keep the *Southern Belle* here until she solves the murder?"

"As far as I know." Williams shrugged. "She won't be able to do that, of course. Mr. Gallister's lawyers will be in front of a judge within the hour if she tries to, getting court orders forcing her to release the boat. Perhaps it won't come to that. We're not due to leave Hannibal until after lunch. With any luck the whole thing will be over by then."

I hoped so. From everything I had heard, the longer it took to solve a murder, the less likelihood the killer would ever be found. And even though I was still a little mad at Ben Webster, I wanted justice to catch up with whoever broke his neck.

Even if it was Mark Lansing?

I didn't know where that thought came from, but it flashed through my head. I tried telling myself that Mark was way too nice to be a murderer, but I knew that things didn't work like that in the real world. You couldn't tell a killer by looking at him.

And Mark was big enough, and in good enough shape, to break somebody's neck in a fight, even if he wasn't a gorilla like Logan Rafferty. He was a man with secrets, too. His late-night visitor and the gun in his shaving kit were proof of that. Maybe he had some even more dangerous secrets.

"I suppose I'll have to make an announcement to the passengers," Captain Williams went on. "If we aren't allowed to leave on schedule, people may need to make arrangements. I'll wait a while before I do it, but I want the passengers to have a chance to call anyone they need to call and let them know they won't be leaving Hannibal when they were supposed to."

That made sense, but I didn't envy him the job. I was sure that once folks heard their plans were going to be disrupted, there would be a lot of angry passengers on board the *Southern Belle.* Chances were they'd be all over the captain and his officers like white on rice, complaining about the delay in returning to St. Louis.

A waiter came over and we ordered breakfast. Captain Williams didn't get up, so it looked like he was going to eat with us. I was a little disappointed. I wanted to talk to Mark in private, as soon as I got the chance.

But not *too* private, I warned myself, just in case he tried to break *my* neck when I started asking questions.

CHAPTER 12

We were just finishing our breakfast when Logan Rafferty came into the dining room. He looked around, spotted the captain, and headed toward us. He didn't look happy to see me, and I knew I wasn't happy to see him.

"That cop is back, Captain," he said as he came up to the table.

"Detective Travis, you mean?"

"Yeah. She wants to see you. I told her to wait in my office, and I'd find you."

"She has good news, I hope?" Even as he asked the question, Williams didn't sound like he really expected to be happy with the answer.

Rafferty glanced at me and Mark. "I don't know," he said. "She didn't tell me anything."

Williams sighed wearily, drank the rest of his coffee, and stood up. "I'll go see what she wants. Thank you, Logan."

They left the dining room together. Mark watched them go, then said, "Rafferty's not the most likable guy in the world, is he?"

"Not hardly," I said. "I feel a little sorry for the captain, though, having to deal with a mess like this."

"Yeah, me too." He looked over at me and went on, "I wonder if we're confined to the boat. If the cops will let us go ashore, maybe we could have a look around Hannibal this morning. Pretend that we're just a couple of tourists."

"That sounds nice," I said. And it did, even though I wasn't sure I fully trusted Mark anymore. I had seen some of the sights in Hannibal the day before, but I'd been looking for Ben Webster at the time and hadn't really taken the time to appreciate any of them. I wasn't going to be surprised, though, if Detective Travis had left an officer or two on duty at the gangway to keep the passengers from leaving the boat.

She wouldn't want any suspects wandering off.

I was about to suggest that we take a stroll along the deck to walk off the food we'd just eaten. That would give me a chance to ask Mark about the mystery woman and the gun. Once I did, that might be the end of any budding friendship between us, but I couldn't help that. I felt like I had to know, especially about the gun.

Before I could make the suggestion, though, Eddie and Louise Kramer came into the dining room. Eddie looked around and then started across the room toward the table where Mark and I sat. He looked like he was fixing to cloud up and rain all over somebody, and since he didn't even know Mark, I figured I was the one about to get caught in the downpour.

Louise trailed after him, looking worried and ineffectual, as usual.

Mark saw them coming and said under his breath, "Uh-oh. This guy doesn't look happy."

"Yeah, and I'm bettin' it's me he's not happy with."

I would have won that bet. Eddie Kramer stalked up to the table and said, "What's this crap I hear about the boat not going back to St. Louis today?"

As usual, his voice was loud enough so that everybody in the room heard what he said. That brought some surprised reactions from the other passengers who were in the dining room. A few of them might have heard rumors about some trouble on the boat, but here was Eddie confirming it in a loud, blustery tone.

All I could do was answer him honestly. "That's a possibility, Mr. Kramer," I said, "but I really don't think—"

"That's not acceptable. We've got a schedule to keep."

"I thought you were on vacation."

"We are. That doesn't mean we don't stick to a schedule. We need to get back to St. Louis. I've got a business to run, you know."

Louise put a hand on his arm. "Eddie . . ." she began.

He shook her off, and I could tell from the way he did it that he had lots of practice.

"What's the cause of this delay?" he demanded. "I want to know who to sue."

"I'm sure there won't be any need to sue anybody. It's still possible that we'll leave Hannibal on schedule this afternoon—"

"We'd better."

Somebody came up behind Eddie and put a hand on his shoulder. Without looking around, he tried to shrug it off and said, "Blast it, Louise—"

But the hand didn't shrug off, and it didn't belong to Louise. Vince Mallory just clamped down tighter and said, "Take it easy, friend. You're jumping the gun here. Ms. Dickinson told you there may not even be a delay in leaving. Why don't you wait and see what happens before you get upset?"

Eddie glared over at him. "Who the hell are you?"

"Just a fellow passenger who thinks it's too early in the morning for a big commotion," Vince said.

Louise looked more worried than ever, and I wondered if she was afraid her husband would take a swing at Vince. Eddie looked like he was considering it, but Vince was just as big as he was and a good twenty years younger. So after a few seconds, Eddie said, "All right, all right already. I just wanted to know what's going on, that's all."

I got to my feet. "I know that, Mr. Kramer, and I don't blame you for being concerned. I think the captain is planning to make an announcement concerning our plans later this morning, and I'm sure if you'll be patient, he'll explain everything then."

"I wasn't counting on being stuck here in Hannibal."

"None of us were," I told him.

Vince let him go and stepped back. Louise seemed to relax slightly, but she still looked skittish. Mark had looked like he was about to stand up when Eddie was on the verge of making a scene, but Vince's arrival had kept that from being necessary. Now all of us waited to see what Eddie was going to do next.

"I need coffee," he muttered. There was a self-service urn on a table against the wall, along with stacked cups and sugar and creamer. He headed toward it.

"I'm going back out on deck, Eddie," Louise called after him. "I think I need some air."

He just grunted, clearly not caring what she did.

Louise looked at Mark, Vince, and me, shrugged in apology, and then left the dining room.

"Thanks," I told Vince. "I reckon he would've gone on gettin' louder and more obnoxious if you hadn't given us a hand."

Vince smiled and shrugged. "No problem. I heard the commotion when I came in and spotted you in the center of it, Ms. Dickinson."

"Do you know Mark Lansing?" I asked.

Vince shook his head. "I don't think we've met." He stuck out his hand. "Vince Mallory. Are you a passenger, too, sir?"

"No, I work on the boat," Mark said as he shook hands with Vince. "Nice to meet you."

"Same here." Vince turned back to me. "Is what that guy said true? We're not heading back to St. Louis when we're supposed to?"

"That's possible," I admitted.

"Is something wrong with the boat?"

"The captain will explain it all later."

Vince grinned. "I get it. You can't talk about it. Well, I don't have to be anywhere at any particular time, so I guess Hannibal is as good a place to be as any. Better than Baghdad or Tikrit, let me tell you."

"You served in Iraq?" Mark asked.

"Yes, sir. I was an MP."

"You did a good job over there."

"Most of us. Thank you, sir."

With a wave, Vince headed for the coffee urn. Eddie Kramer had already filled his cup and found an empty table in a corner. He watched Vince with a scowl on his face, but Vince ignored him.

"Did you hear that kid?" Mark asked as we sat down again.

"What about him?"

"He called me sir."

"So?"

He smiled and shook his head. "You know you're getting old when grown men start calling you sir."

"Oh, that's probably just because he was in the army. He's probably in the habit of calling everybody sir or ma'am."

"He didn't call you ma'am," Mark pointed out.

"Maybe not, but I wouldn't be surprised if he did. And it wouldn't bother me, either." I gestured toward my head. "If you look close—and I wouldn't necessarily advise it—you might find a gray hair or two up here. I figure I've earned every one of 'em."

He chuckled. "I've got to go tend to some business, but I hope I'll see you later. I'll call you, and we'll make a break for it."

"Go see the Mark Twain Museum, you mean?"

"Hey, in my line of work, it'd be a business expense, now wouldn't it?"

I smiled as he stood up. I wondered if he was going to lean over and kiss me before he left.

He didn't. Just as well. I didn't need folks gossiping about me.

I had some coffee left in my cup. I lingered over the last of it. While I was doing that, Vince came over and used his coffee cup to indicate one of the empty chairs as he raised his eyebrows. I smiled and said, "Sit."

He sat. A look of concern replaced the friendly expression on his face.

"I overheard some people talking. They said someone was killed on board yesterday and that the reason we can't leave is because of an investigation that's going on. Is that true?"

I took a deep breath. "You believe in puttin' it right out there, don't you?"

"I've never been one to beat around the bush."

I hesitated for a second, then made up my mind to tell him the truth. "Yes, someone was killed."

"An accident?"

"No. He was murdered."

Vince let out a low whistle of surprise. "I thought maybe we'd have the NTSB coming on board, or some agency like that. I guess the cops are in charge, though."

"Yeah, a detective from the Hannibal police force is handling the investigation. Detective Travis."

"I wonder if he could use a hand."

"She," I said, then frowned. "What do you mean by that?"

"I told you, I was military police. I have a little experience with murder investigations. Maybe I should offer my services to Detective Travis."

Remembering Travis's severe demeanor from the night before, I said, "I don't reckon that'd be a good idea. I think she's on top of the situation."

Vince shrugged. "You're probably right. I've thought about going into police work, if I don't go back to grad school." He chuckled. "But I guess nobody ever volunteers to be an amateur detective, do they?"

I hadn't exactly volunteered when folks started dying on that plantation outside of Atlanta the year before. . . .

I pushed that thought out of my head and said, "I'm sure you'll figure out what you want to do with your life. Shoot, you're so young you don't have to worry about rushin' into anything."

"Maybe so."

We chatted for a few more minutes, and then my phone rang. I said, "Excuse me," to Vince and took it out of my purse. Melissa and Luke's home number was in the display. "My daughter."

"I'll see you later, ma'am," Vince said with a friendly grin as he got up from the table. He waved and headed for the doors leading out onto the desk.

Ma'am? Mark was right. It did sort of throw me.

I answered the phone, and Melissa's worried voice said, "Mom, are you all right?"

"Of course I'm all right," I told her. "Why wouldn't I be?"

"It just came on the news that there was a murder on board the *Southern Belle* yesterday."

Well, if it had made the TV, the proverbial doo-doo was about to hit the proverbial fan, I thought. Everybody on board would know before Captain Williams got a chance to make his announcement.

"Is it true?" Melissa went on.

"I'm afraid so."

"Was the victim one of our clients?"

"Yep."

"Oh, no," she moaned. "More bad publicity. We were just putting that whole plantation business behind us."

"Yeah, it sure was inconsiderate of Mr. Webster to go and get himself killed on one of our tours, wasn't it?"

"I didn't mean it like that," Melissa said quickly. "Of course I'm sorry it happened. Is there anything I can do to help?"

"As a matter of fact, there is. Somebody broke into my cabin last night and stole my laptop—"

"That's terrible! Were you there?"

"No, it happened while I was out, thank goodness. But I'll need the serial number and all the other information you can get me about the computer for the police report."

"Of course. When I get to the office, I'll e-mail it to— No, I guess I won't, will I?"

"Just call me," I told her. "Check the computer for everything we have on Ben Webster, too."

"The murder victim?"

"That's right. The detective in charge of the case asked me for his credit card number and anything else we have on file."

"I'll take care of it as soon as I get to the office, Mom," Melissa promised. "I don't imagine we'll have much that's useful to the police, though. Is there anything else?"

I hesitated, then said, "Find out anything you can about Eddie and Louise Kramer, too."

"I remember the names. . . . Do they have anything to do with the murder?"

"No, no," I said. "I'm just curious about them."

I wasn't sure why I asked her about the Kramers. They had no connection at all with Ben Webster except that they were on the same boat. But Eddie was big, and he had a temper. . . .

There was no point in going down that road,

I told myself. Anyway, Melissa probably wouldn't find anything in the computer except their basic info.

I assured her again that I was all right, told her to give my love to Luke, and said that I'd talk to her later after she got to the office. The coffee that was still in my cup was cold by now, but I drank it anyway and then left the dining room, unsure what I would do next. I was still mighty curious about the woman who had come to Mark's cabin in the middle of the night, as well as the gun, but circumstances had conspired to keep me from asking him about them.

Maybe I would go back up to his cabin and see if he was there. It wasn't as public a place as the dining room, but I couldn't really bring myself to believe that I'd be in any danger from him.

I took the stairs to the second deck. When I got there I realized I'd have to go past the AUTHORIZED PERSONNEL ONLY sign to get to Mark's cabin. I hesitated—old habits are hard to break, and I'd always been the sort of girl who follows the rules—and while I was standing there I saw the door to Mark's cabin open.

A woman stepped out. I saw blond hair and realized with a shock that I knew her. I had seen her fleeing down the deck the night before, but that wasn't the only place. In fact, I had seen her a short time earlier in the dining room.

Louise Kramer.

It got worse, though. I stepped back hurriedly around the corner at the end of the deck,

edging forward just enough so that I could see
along the line of cabins. Mark came out of his
cabin and gave Louise a hug, holding her
tightly.

Whether I liked it or not, I had to admit to
myself that Mark Lansing was as sorry as a two-
dollar watch.

CHAPTER 13

After a long moment, Mark let go of Louise, moved back a step, and patted her on the shoulder. At least he didn't kiss her. Not out here in the open, anyway. Who knew what had gone on inside the cabin? Not me, and I didn't want to think about it. Even if Louise's husband was a jerk, she was still *married*, for gosh sake.

She was about to turn away from Mark and come in my direction. I didn't want her to see me, so I ducked into the stairway and headed back down to the first deck. It seemed like my efforts to question Mark were doomed to failure, but despite that I had just found out one of the things I wanted to know: the identity of the woman who had come to his cabin the night before.

And I almost wished that I hadn't.

That still didn't explain why he had a gun hidden in his shaving kit. Maybe to protect himself from jealous husbands.

By the time I reached the first deck, another

question had occurred to me. Had Mark known Louise Kramer before the cruise? He lived in St. Louis, he had told me. I couldn't remember where the Kramers were from, although I was sure I had seen the information when we were processing their booking in the office. I was glad now that I had told Melissa to get what information she could about them, although I wasn't sure what, if anything, I could do with it.

If Mark hadn't known Louise, that meant he was a mighty fast worker, getting her to come to his cabin in the middle of the night like that.

And where exactly were you *at the time, missy?* I asked myself. In Mark Lansing's cabin.

I leaned against the wall or bulkhead or whatever you call it and closed my eyes as the wheels, like those of the bus in the song I used to sing to Melissa when she was a baby, went round and round in my head. If Mark was expecting Louise to show up at his cabin, why in heaven's name had he asked me to spend the night there? Had he forgotten that he had an illicit rendezvous planned? That didn't seem very likely. The whole thing didn't make any sense.

I must have stood there with my eyes closed for longer than the second or so I intended, because the next thing I knew a familiar voice was asking me, "Are you all right, Ms. Dickinson?"

Oh, no. This was just too much. I opened my eyes and saw Louise Kramer standing there with a concerned look on her face.

I fought down the impulse to ask her what the heck was wrong with her, carrying on like that with a man who wasn't her husband. Instead I managed to say, "Yeah, I'm okay. Just tired from everything that's been goin' on the past couple of days."

"I can understand that. It's just terrible about that young man being murdered." She leaned closer to me and lowered her voice. "He *was* murdered, wasn't he? That's what I've heard."

"I'm afraid so." There was no point in trying to keep the circumstances of Ben Webster's death quiet now.

"It's such a tragedy when a . . . a young person's life is cut short like that," she said, her voice choking with emotion. I saw tears spring into shining life in her eyes as she repeated, "Such a tragedy."

She looked like she was taking it pretty hard, considering that she hadn't even known Webster. I was trying to come up with something consoling to say, even though I was still upset about the whole Mark thing, when the phone in my pants pocket rang.

I took it out, saw that it was the office calling, and said, "Excuse me," to Louise. She just nodded and wiped at one of her eyes.

"Mom," Melissa said when I answered, "are you where you can write down that information about your computer?"

"No, not really," I said. "I can call you back in a minute—"

"Hang on, Mom, I have some stuff here you might need to know. It's about the Kramers."

That caught my interest. I summoned up a smile for Louise to keep her there, then told Melissa, "All right, go ahead."

"I checked our records first, of course, but all that was there was their credit card number and their contact information."

"What's that last part again?" I asked, remembering my question about whether or not Mark and Louise had known each other before the cruise.

"You mean the address?"

"Just the last part will do," I told her.

"The town where they live? That would be Kennett, Missouri."

I was familiar with Kennett. It was a small city way down in the boot heel of Missouri. I recalled Mark saying that he was born in that area but raised in St. Louis. So it was conceivable that Mark and Louise had known each other in the past, maybe as kids. They were about the same age, after all.

"Go on," I told Melissa.

"I wasn't sure why you wanted to know about them, but I knew it would only take a minute to search their names on the Internet. That's where I found the archived newspaper stories about the murder."

My fingers tightened on the phone in surprise. I managed to keep the smile on my face, but I imagine it was starting to look a little hollow right about then. I swallowed and said, "What about it?"

I was waiting for Melissa to tell me that the police had charged Eddie Kramer with murdering one of his wife's lovers. But the truth was a lot more painful than that.

"Their daughter was killed," Melissa said.

I swallowed hard again to hide the shock I felt. "Really?"

"Yes. Her name was Hannah. She was twenty-two. But get this, Mom . . . she was killed on the *Southern Belle*. It happened one year ago today . . . and the police never found the murderer."

I was as dizzy as I'd been the night before when I was full of champagne and no food. The deck seemed to be spinning around me. The phone was my lifeline, and I clung to it.

"Go on," I said.

"Hannah Kramer worked on the *Southern Belle*. She was a cocktail waitress in the casino. Someone hit her on the head and threw her into one of the paddlewheels."

I couldn't help myself. That was so gruesome I had to mutter, "Oh, Lord." The fact that I was standing there next to Hannah Kramer's mother didn't help matters.

One year ago today, Melissa had said. What sort of people went off on a vacation on the one-year anniversary of their child's murder?

What sort of mother would carry on an affair at a time like that?

I took a breath and told myself not to be so judgmental. My shoes are my own. I don't walk in anybody else's. But I can imagine it when I try.

"Yeah," Melissa continued, "it could have been even worse than it was if somebody hadn't spotted the body right away and raised the alarm. They were able to stop the boat before the paddlewheel, uh, did too much damage."

I had to be careful how I phrased my questions, what with Louise standing right there. "How do they know that's what the situation was?"

"Murder, you mean? At first they thought she must have fallen overboard by accident, but at the autopsy they found metal fragments in one of the wounds on her head. Somebody hit her with a piece of pipe. From that the cops decided that someone knocked her out first and then *threw* her into the paddlewheel. The killer probably figured that the damage from the paddlewheel would cover up the evidence of the other blow, but it didn't work out that way."

I knew Melissa was probably paraphrasing the newspaper stories about the murder that she'd found on the Internet, but it was still chilling to hear the matter-of-fact way she said it. I didn't blame her, of course; she hadn't known Hannah Kramer and had no way of knowing that I was with Hannah's mother.

"Go on," I told her.

"That's really all there is to tell. The State Police investigated the case, of course, but they never made any arrests. The theory is that someone on the boat tried to rob her, but hit her too hard and then panicked and threw her over the side when they saw she was dead. That makes sense, I guess."

It did, and for all I knew, that was exactly what had happened. I looked at Louise and saw that she was still wiping tears away. The fact that Ben Webster had been murdered one day before the one-year anniversary of her daughter's death must have gotten to her.

That didn't explain what she and her husband were doing on this cruise, or why Louise
was carrying on with Mark Lansing, but those
were questions that Melissa couldn't answer no
matter how much searching she did on the Internet.

Only Louise had those answers.

"Well, thanks for letting me know," I told
Melissa. "I'll call you back in a little while to get
those numbers."

"Okay. Let me know if there's anything else I
can do to help. Do you have any idea when
you'll be able to get back home?"

"Not a clue," I said.

As I closed the phone and slipped it back into
my pocket, I went on to Louise, "Sorry for the
interruption. That was my office. My daughter,
actually. She works for me."

Maybe I imagined it, or maybe I noticed it because of what I had just found out, but I thought
Louise flinched the tiniest bit at the word
daughter. Just one more reminder of her loss.
But she smiled and said, "That must be nice. To
have your daughter working for you, I mean."

"Yeah, she's good at runnin' the office, and
her husband helps me with the tours. He didn't
come along on this one because I figured I
could handle it without any trouble."

"You couldn't have known about . . . about
what was going to happen. Tragedies usually
come out of nowhere. That's one of the most
awful things about them, the way they take you
by such surprise. I mean, you're just going along
with your life, and then suddenly . . . suddenly

everything that matters to you is ripped out from under you. . . ."

I could see it happening. She was talking herself into a breakdown right in front of me, and there wasn't a darn thing I could do to stop it. As her voice trailed off, the waterworks came on full blast. Tears began to roll down her cheeks as she shuddered, and before I could move, she stepped forward, put her arms around me, and started to sob against my shoulder.

As much as the idea of her carrying on with Mark Lansing bothered me, I couldn't push her away. As one mother to another, all I could do was hug her, pat her on the back, and let her cry. She had no idea that I knew what had happened to her daughter, of course, but I did know and I couldn't help but sympathize.

After a minute she started to recover her composure. "I'm so sorry," she said as she stepped back and wiped the back of her hand across her sniffly nose. "I . . . I don't know what's wrong with me. I didn't mean to get so emotional."

"That's all right," I told her. "I can tell something's really botherin' you. Would you like to go get a cup of coffee and talk about it?"

I didn't make the suggestion because I thought it would be a good opportunity to ask her some questions. I really didn't. Honestly, sharing some sympathy along with the coffee was the only thing I had in mind when the words came out of my mouth.

But no sooner had I said them than I realized

that this might be a chance to find out more about what was going on between her and Mark. Louise seemed to like me, and she might open up to me. I felt a little cold and calculating, but I wasn't going to pass up the opportunity.

"Are . . . are you sure?" she asked. "I know you must have more important things to do. . . ."

I shook my head. "Not at all. This is plenty important." I took her arm. "Come with me to the dining room. I reckon you'll feel better if you get some of it out."

She managed a wan smile. "You know, I think that I will. Feel better, that is."

It was still early enough that quite a few people were having breakfast in the dining room, but after Louise and I helped ourselves to coffee, we found an empty table in a corner where not too many folks could overhear what we were saying. Louise began, "You don't have any way of knowing this, Ms. Dickinson—"

I broke in, "Please, call me Delilah."

"All right. Delilah." She smiled. "It's such a pretty name. Of course, in the Bible Delilah tempted Samson and betrayed him."

"I don't see any long-haired fellas around here. Anyway, I reckon my temptress days are behind me."

"Oh, I wouldn't say that. You're still a very attractive woman."

Mark had seemed to think so, I thought, but I didn't say it. Instead I said, "Go ahead and tell me what's botherin' you, if you want to."

"I hardly know how to say it."

"In my experience, if something's painful, it's best to just come right out with it."

"I suppose you're right." Louise took a deep breath. "Eddie and I didn't come on this cruise just for a vacation. Oh, it's true that he needed to get away from his business. He's so driven that I'll try anything to get him to relax. He's thrown himself into his work so hard for the past year that I'm afraid he's going to have a heart attack or something. But I understand why he does it. That's the only way he can cope. He has to keep himself so busy because he can't allow himself to think about . . . about what happened."

She stopped and took a sip of coffee. I didn't say anything. I sensed that the best thing for me to do now was to keep quiet and let Louise Kramer tell her story however she wanted to.

"You must be wondering what I'm talking about," she said with a sad, tiny smile. "You'd be even more surprised if you knew the real reason *I* came on this cruise."

To fool around with Mark Lansing? I thought, but again I didn't say it. Instead I suggested, "Why don't you tell me?"

Louise looked straight at me across the table and nodded. "All right, I will. I came on this cruise, Delilah, because I want to kill someone."

CHAPTER 14

"See?" she went on. "I told you you'd be shocked."

I realized I was staring. I forced myself to stop it. I shook my head and said, "I reckon there's got to be more to it than that. You don't strike me as the bloodthirsty type, Louise."

"Oh, that's where you're wrong. Under the right circumstances, I think I could be very bloodthirsty indeed. If I had the person who killed my little girl right in front of me, and a gun in my hand, I could . . . I could . . ."

She wasn't able to go on just then. Instead she pushed her coffee cup aside and put her hands over her face for a moment. She looked completely grief stricken.

When she lowered her hands, she said, "Now you really do deserve an explanation. You must think I'm a crazy person."

"Not at all," I told her, but to tell the truth, I wasn't a hundred percent convinced of that.

"You see, Delilah, one year ago . . . one year

ago *today* . . . my daughter, Hannah, was killed on this riverboat. This exact same riverboat. Someone murdered her."

I tried to look as surprised as I would have been if Melissa hadn't told me the same thing a few minutes earlier. I didn't have to fake the sympathy I felt as I reached across the table, clasped Louise's hand, and murmured, "That's terrible."

"You don't know how terrible it is. When you get back to Atlanta, you give your daughter a great big hug and tell her how much you love her. Do that every day."

"You know, I think maybe I should."

Louise nodded. "I wish I'd been able to do that one more time. Just one more time, so Hannah would know."

"I'm sure she did."

"I hope so." She sighed. "Anyway, when I said I wanted to kill someone, I meant that I'd like to find whoever murdered Hannah and . . . well, I can't say even the score, because you don't keep score with your loved ones' lives. . . ."

"Of course not."

"But see that justice is done, I guess you'd say. And to me, there can be no justice while the person responsible for Hannah's death is still drawing breath."

She had stopped crying. Her eyes burned with the desire for vengeance now. I had no trouble believing that if she had a gun and knew who had killed her daughter, she wouldn't hesitate to shoot whoever it was.

I had to pretend that I didn't know any of the

story's details. "Tell me about it," I said. "It might help."

"I'm not sure anything will help, but . . . all right. It started a couple of years ago when Hannah and her father had a terrible argument." That sad smile came back on her face. "Eddie's not the easiest man in the world to live with. He hasn't been for me, and he wasn't for Hannah, although he did love her a great deal. But they just didn't get along, and when they argued that last time, Eddie told her she could move out if she didn't like the way he did things. She was twenty-one then, so it was her decision. She didn't just leave home, though. She moved all the way to St. Louis."

"Where do you live?" I asked, even though I already knew the answer.

"A little town called Kennett."

I nodded. "I've heard of it."

"I worried so much about her, but she seemed to be happy. She met a man she liked, and she got a job, here on this boat. She worked in the casino as a waitress." Louise shrugged. "It wasn't really what you'd call a good job, but she hoped it would lead to better things."

"I'm sure it would have."

"If she'd ever had the chance . . . But then someone . . . someone . . ."

Even though I wanted to hear the story from her, the pain in her eyes was so stark I couldn't help but feel sorry for her. "You don't have to go on if it's too hard," I told her. "I understand. And this is really none of my business."

"Yes, it is," Louise said. "Because Eddie and I

came on this cruise under false pretenses. Or at least *I* did, anyway."

"What do you mean, false pretenses?"

"Like you said, it's not as painful to just come right out with it. After Hannah had been working on the riverboat for a while, someone hit her on the head and threw her overboard. She was caught in one of the paddlewheels."

"Good Lord," I muttered, and I didn't have to fake the horror I felt at hearing it again, this time from the mouth of the murdered girl's mother.

"Yes, it was terrible," Louise agreed. "The police told us that the blow to the head probably would have been fatal, even if she hadn't gone overboard. The killer was just . . . making sure, I suppose you'd say."

All I could do was shake my head in sympathy and wait for her to go on.

"The police investigated but never made any arrests. I don't think they ever even had any strong suspects. I'm not sure they even cared that much about solving the case."

"Oh, I imagine they did. They just didn't have any leads, I expect."

"Well, I have a lead," Louise said. "Hannah had told me less than a week earlier that she'd had some sort of trouble with someone else who worked on the boat. But she didn't say who or what it was about, and when I told the police, they told me they had questioned all the other employees and everyone said Hannah got along just fine with everyone else. They claimed not to know what I was talking about."

"But you think one of the crew killed her?"

Louise nodded. "I'm convinced of it. I just don't have any proof or anything to tell me which one. So I did the only thing I could." She hesitated. "You won't tell anyone about this?"

"There's nobody I'd tell," I assured her.

"I hired a private detective," Louise said. "An old acquaintance of mine. You know him. Mark Lansing."

That just about floored me. I tried to keep the surprise off my face, but I'm not sure I managed. "Mark?" I repeated. "Mark is a private detective?"

Louise nodded. "His mother and my mother are good friends and have been since we were kids. I've kept up with him that way, even after he moved to St. Louis."

"Let me get this straight. If he's a private detective, what's he doing pretending to be Mark Twain?"

Louise leaned forward over the table and lowered her voice to a conspiratorial tone. "He's undercover."

Well, that made sense, I supposed. If Louise had hired Mark to investigate her daughter's murder, and she thought that someone who worked on the *Southern Belle* was responsible for it, then Mark would be able to find out more if everyone on the boat thought he was just an actor playing Mark Twain. The killer wouldn't suspect him of being a detective.

That explained the gun in his shaving kit, too. I'm no expert on such things, but it seemed likely to me that a private detective would have a license to carry a gun.

And the fact that Mark and Louise were old friends, as I had thought they might be once I found out where Louise was from, even explained the hug. There wasn't any hanky-panky going on between them, and she had probably come to his cabin the night before to see if he had uncovered anything important in his investigation.

At least, I hoped that was the case.

I mulled all that over in my head for a couple of seconds, then said, "So you and Eddie hired Mark—"

"No," Louise interrupted. "*I* hired Mark. Eddie doesn't know anything about it. He thinks . . . he thinks that we should just move on, that Hannah's murder will never be solved and we just have to accept it. I was barely able to talk him into taking this cruise with me. I told him it was going to be my way of . . . of saying good-bye to her."

"But you're really hoping that Mark will find out who killed her?"

She nodded. "That's right. I realize, after all this time, the odds are against it. But I have to keep hoping, you see. I have to keep hoping for justice."

I understood. I couldn't imagine the pain and grief she must have experienced, of course, since I'd never been through anything like that in my life and hoped that I never would. But I could see in her eyes how important it was to her that Hannah's killer be found.

"Does your husband even know Mark?" I asked. Eddie hadn't acted like it when we were all in the dining room earlier.

Louise shook her head. "He's heard me talk about him, but they've never actually met."

I was a little annoyed. Mark Lansing had told me that he was a lawyer before he became an actor and got the job as Mark Twain. I supposed I could forgive a fib like that, since it was in the line of duty, so to speak, but I was irked anyway. He could have told me the truth.

And just why would he do that? I asked myself. Less than twenty-four hours earlier, he hadn't known me from Adam—or Eve. Even though I was convinced he actually liked me—that hadn't been an act—his first responsibility was to his client. I could understand that feeling, since I felt it myself toward the folks who went on my tours.

Still, I intended to have a talk with Mr. Mark Lansing and inform him that I knew the truth now. From here on out I expected him to shoot straight with me.

"Anyway," Louise went on, "you can see why I was upset when I heard about Mr. Webster. Even though I didn't know him, to have another young person killed here on the same boat, on almost the same day . . . it was just too much for me. That's why I lost it for a minute. I'm sorry, Delilah."

"Nothin' to apologize for," I told her. "You had every reason to be upset. I hope that talkin' about it has made you feel better."

She smiled, and it wasn't quite as sad this

time. "I believe it has, a little bit. But now I've added to your burden."

"Not at all. Has, uh, Mark found out anything?"

Louise sighed. "I'm afraid not. A lot of the people who worked on the boat with Hannah are still here, but some of them have left in the past year, of course. We may never be able to track down all of them. But my instincts tell me that the killer is still here. A mother's instincts can't be wrong, can they?"

All the time, I thought. I knew that from bitter experience. No matter how good a kid was—and Melissa was a mighty good one—there were going to be times when they'd let you down when you'd least expect it. Probably the same held true about being a parent.

"Mark's been around the boat for several days now," Louise went on, "but he told me this morning that he hasn't found anyone who had trouble with Hannah before she was killed. The only possible clue he's come up with is finding one of the dealers in the casino who knew Hannah and said she was worried about something a couple of days before she died. He said she was so nervous she was sick to her stomach."

"Did she get like that very often?"

"Not at all. Hannah was always very healthy."

I didn't know what that meant, if anything, but I filed it away in my brain, anyway.

"So you talked to Mark about the case this morning?" I asked. Louise didn't know that I had seen her coming out of his cabin, and I figured I probably wouldn't tell her. That would just complicate things.

"Yes, I went up to his cabin for a few minutes after we saw the two of you in the dining room. I was able to catch his eye there, and I guess he understood that I wanted to talk." Her mouth tightened. "I was going to talk to him last night. I even slipped up to his cabin after Eddie had gone to sleep. Once Eddie's good and asleep you can't wake him with a bullhorn. But Mark had company."

I swallowed. "Really?" I managed to say.

"That's right. He gave me a key to his cabin, but when I started to let myself in, the chain was on . . . and there was a woman in there."

"Do tell," I murmured.

"Of course, Mark's private life is his own business, and I don't expect him to be working on Hannah's case twenty-four hours a day. I know it shouldn't bother me that he's already made a conquest. . . ."

I wouldn't have gone so far as to call it *that*.

"But I guess it does, a little," she went on. "I'm curious, too, if it's someone who works on the boat or one of the passengers. If it's one of the passengers, someone Mark didn't even meet until yesterday . . . well, I'm no prude, but that seems like moving awfully fast to me."

I couldn't argue with her there. It seemed mighty fast to me, too. But there had been extenuating circumstances, I told myself, and anyway, nothing had happened. All I'd done was borrow Mark's cabin for the night. He hadn't even been there.

"Did you ask him about it this morning?"

Louise shook her head. "Oh, no, I couldn't have. I was too embarrassed. And he didn't bring it up, so either he was asleep and his girlfriend didn't tell him about me showing up at his cabin, or else he was too ashamed to admit it."

I knew the truth. Mark didn't know a thing about her coming to his cabin the night before. And it would be better all around, I told myself, if things stayed that way.

Louise drank some more of her coffee, then said, "My, I've really poured my heart out to you, haven't I? I hope I haven't bored you too much."

"Not at all," I assured her. "And I'm so sorry for your loss, Louise." I added the thing that people always say at times of tragedy. "If there's anything I can do to help . . ."

"You've been a good listener." She squeezed my hand. "That's enough. Unless you can figure out who killed my daughter and tell the police."

She didn't know about what had happened on the plantation the year before. At least, I figured she didn't. The case had gotten some national publicity, but not much. My fifteen minutes of fame, or notoriety, as the case may be, were long since over.

"I'll leave that to trained detectives like Mark," I said.

Louise stood up. "I'd better go find Eddie. He was going to make some calls to his office, but I'm sure he's done with that by now. He's probably wandering around the boat looking for me, and I don't want him getting into any trouble."

She said that like a woman who was used to her husband running the risk of getting into trouble anytime he was out on his own. Given Eddie Kramer's volatile temper, I could understand why.

That thought brought me right back to Ben Webster. I didn't know anything about him, but I didn't see how there could be any connection between him and Hannah Kramer's murder. If there *was* a connection, though, and Eddie somehow found out about it . . . well, I could see him breaking Ben's neck. I didn't have any trouble visualizing that at all.

"If you need any help, here I am," I told her as I stood up, too. "You just let me know."

"Thanks. I think you have the makings of a good friend, Delilah."

"I hope so."

She smiled and left the dining room. I picked up my coffee, finished it off, then decided I'd go look up Mark. We needed to have a talk and get some things out in the open between us.

As I stepped out onto the deck, I noticed a big, dark blue car pulling into the parking area adjacent to the dock. It stopped in one of the handicapped spaces—and didn't have a handicapped sticker or hanger, I noticed—and a man in a uniform of some sort got out from behind the wheel. He was a chauffeur, not a cop, I realized as he opened the car's rear door to let a man in what looked like an extremely expensive charcoal gray suit climb out.

The man didn't acknowledge the chauffeur, just started toward the gangway leading to the riverboat's main deck. He was in his fifties, I guessed, stocky and broad shouldered, like he'd been an athlete in his younger years and was still fairly fit for his age. Brown hair starting to turn gray topped a beefy face.

Captain Williams appeared on deck just as the newcomer reached the bottom of the gangway. The captain waited there, a worried frown on his face, as the man strode on board in a no-nonsense manner. He certainly didn't ask Williams for permission to come aboard, either, although I didn't know if that was customary on a riverboat.

There was a good reason for that omission, too. Captain Williams said, "Mr. Gallister. I didn't know you were coming up to Hannibal."

"Someone's got to straighten out this mess, Captain," the newcomer said, "and as the owner of this boat, I hereby appoint myself."

So that was Charles Gallister, I thought, real estate mogul and owner of the *Southern Belle*.

CHAPTER 15

Gallister looked like the successful businessman he was. Up close I could tell that his
suit probably cost even more than I had thought
at first, and I didn't want to think about what the
Italian shoes on his feet or the silk tie knotted
around his throat must have set him back.
Chances were, Gallister himself didn't know
how much they cost and wouldn't care if he did
know. Men such as him didn't worry about the
price of things. They just bought what they
needed—or wanted.

Don't get the idea that I disliked him on sight
just because he was rich. That's not really true.
I'm like everybody else. I'd like to be rich myself
one of these days. The reason I didn't care for
Charles Gallister was that he struck me as arro-
gant, and I guess as successful as he was, he had
every reason to be.

Gallister and Captain Williams started toward
the nearest set of stairs. Williams said, "We'll go

up to the pilothouse and talk, sir. I can fill you in on the situation."

Gallister just nodded curtly. They went up the stairs.

I headed for the salon. I didn't know where I would find Mark, but that seemed as good a place to start looking as any.

He wasn't in the salon. I checked the dining room again, although I didn't think he would have returned there so soon, and sure enough, he wasn't there, either.

That left his cabin. I went there, unhooking the chain and venturing past the warning sign, but he didn't answer my knock and didn't respond when I called his name through the door. I figured he must still be on the boat, but I didn't know where else to look.

"Ms. Dickinson?" a man's voice said. "You need some help?"

I turned to see Vince Mallory at the bottom of the stairs leading to the third deck. I shook my head and said, "No, I was just looking for Mr. Lansing."

Vince probably wondered why I'd gone into an area that was off limits to passengers, but if he did, he didn't say anything about it. Instead he pointed a thumb toward the third deck and said, "I'm afraid I haven't seen Mr. Lansing, but I was about to go up to the observation area. Would you like to join me?"

"Might as well," I said, since I couldn't find Mark. Then I realized how that might sound to Vince and added hurriedly, "I didn't mean to seem unenthusiastic—"

"Hey, that's all right," he broke in with a grin. "No offense taken. I'll be glad for the company."

I went around the chain, rehooked it, and joined Vince at the stairs. We went up side by side, and when we reached the landing on the third deck, we turned right toward the observation area at the bow. Built-in benches with storage areas for purses and things like that underneath them followed along the curving railing.

Each deck was set back from the deck below it, so from up here we could see part of the second deck and the main deck, as well as the dock and most of Hannibal with the gently rolling green hills behind it to the west. It was a beautiful scene, pure Americana. With the people in period costume, including the faux Tom Sawyer and Becky Thatcher, strolling along the streets of Hannibal, I could almost believe the town had gone back in time.

Vince and I sat down on one of the benches. He had a camera bag slung over one shoulder. He reached into the bag, brought out a digital camera, and started taking shots of the riverboat and Hannibal. In between pressing the shutter, he said, "I can see why people like to come here. You can look at the world the way it used to be and forget about all the bad things, at least for a little while."

I heard a touch of sadness in his voice I hadn't noticed there any of the other times I'd talked to him. "You said you'd been in Iraq, didn't you?"

"That's right."

"I reckon you must've seen some pretty rotten stuff over there."

He nodded. "That's true. Even now you run across reminders of how brutal people can be to each other. But that's not just true overseas. People hurt each other all the time, everywhere. Sometimes it's intentional, sometimes it's not. And all you can do is try to embrace the good times and hang on to them for as long as you can."

"That's pretty profound. . . ."

"For a kid, you mean?" he asked with a laugh.

"No, I didn't mean it that way," I said.

"Oh, don't worry, Ms. Dickinson. It doesn't bother me when people point out how young I am. The thing is, when you consider a person's years, you have no way of knowing how old their soul is."

"That's true," I agreed. "I like to think I have a young soul."

He looked over at me, and after a moment he nodded. "I believe you do. I think you have a lot of vitality and compassion and humor in you."

The depth of emotion in his voice surprised me. I said, "Wait a minute. You're not flirtin' with me, are you? Because young soul or not, I'm still old enough to be your . . . aunt."

Vince grinned. "No, not at all. But I do enjoy your company, Ms. Dickinson. You remind me a little of my mom."

Well, that took most of the wind out of my sails, let me tell you. At the same time, I was glad Vince wasn't flirting with me. My feelings were confused enough about Mark. Not to mention I was still upset about Ben Webster's murder. I didn't need anything else on my plate right now.

"I'll take that as a compliment," I told him.

"That's the way I meant it. I'm just sorry . . ."

"What?" I said when his voice trailed off. "What are you sorry about?"

He grinned and shook his head. "Nothing. Just that I started to get all maudlin on you. Look around us." He waved an arm at our surroundings. "Despite all the trouble in the world, it's a beautiful day. I think I'm just going to sit here and enjoy it for a while."

"All right." I took that as my cue to leave.

As I stood up, he asked, "Have you heard anything about when we'll be able to start downriver?"

I shook my head. "Not a word." Movement on the dock caught my eye. I saw Detective Travis step out of a car that had just pulled up and parked. "Maybe I can find out, though."

I lifted a hand to wave good-bye and headed back down the stairs. By the time I reached the main deck, Detective Travis had come on board. I intercepted her.

"Good mornin', Detective."

She nodded. "Ms. Dickinson."

"Any progress on the case?"

"I can't really talk about that," she said.

"Well, do you know when the riverboat can start back to St. Louis?"

"That's not something I can discuss, either."

"Well, what *can* you tell me?"

I saw a flash of irritation in her eyes. "That you're interfering with a police officer."

I held my hands up, palms out, and backed away. "Sorry. I didn't mean to cause a problem. It's just that some of my clients have asked me about it this morning and it's my job to make their trip as pleasant as I can."

"Then you failed with Ben Webster, didn't you?"

I thought that was a cheap shot, and even though I don't like people talking about how I must have a hot temper because of my red hair, sometimes it's more true than I'd like to admit. I said, "I can see why you'd be worried. You don't want a second unsolved murder on this boat, do you?"

Sometimes my mouth runs ahead of my brain, too. I saw the look of surprise that came over Detective Travis's face for a second. Then she asked in a sharp voice, "What do you know about another murder?"

What had happened to Hannah Kramer was no secret. Melissa had found out about it through a simple Internet search, even before Louise had spilled her guts to me. But if I'd been thinking, I wouldn't have brought up the subject with Travis. With a murder investigation going on, nobody wants to draw any more attention from the cops than he or she absolutely has to.

I didn't have to answer Travis's question just then, however, because a man's voice behind me said, "Detective, I want to speak to you."

I looked back over my shoulder and saw Charles Gallister coming along the deck toward us, trailed by a concerned-looking Captain Williams.

Travis said, "Excuse me? Who are you?"

"Charles Gallister. I own this boat."

He said it with a note of pride in his voice that didn't quite come across as pompous. Almost, though.

"Then I'm sure Captain Williams has informed you of the crime that took place on board yesterday," Travis said.

"He certainly has. He also tells me that you refuse to let the *Southern Belle* proceed back to St. Louis on schedule."

"This boat is a crime scene, Mr. Gallister. The police like to keep crime scenes as secure as possible until the initial investigation is complete." Travis took me by surprise by smiling. "We're funny that way."

Gallister made an encompassing gesture. "You can't just declare that the entire boat is the crime scene. That's absurd."

"Not really," Travis insisted. "We don't know where Mr. Webster was murdered, but we know that he had been dead for several hours when he was found. That means he was killed while the *Southern Belle* was still cruising upriver. The crime has to have taken place *somewhere* on this boat . . . unless you expect us to believe that Webster was taken off the boat, killed somewhere else, and then returned to the *Southern Belle,* where his body was stuffed in that storage locker."

Gallister frowned. "That's ridiculous."

"Yes, sir. We think so, too."

Gallister wasn't going to give up. "Nevertheless, I'm sure that your crime scene people have been all over the place where the body was found. You've documented everything there is to document. There's no reason to hold the boat here."

"Other than the fact that all of the suspects in the case are on board." Travis inclined her head toward the uniformed cops who were standing beside the gangway. "My men have been here all night. No one has gotten off the boat, and the only ones who have gotten on are passengers returning from Hannibal . . . and you."

"Me?" Gallister's eyes widened. "Surely you don't consider *me* a suspect in this horrible crime, Detective."

"No, sir." Travis smiled faintly again. "I've already checked on your whereabouts yesterday. Your presence in St. Louis is well accounted for."

Gallister snorted. "I should hope so. Why, I never even heard of that young man who was killed."

"Ben Webster. That was his name."

"Well, I'm sorry about what happened to him, of course. But I have a boat full of passengers who want to get on with their lives." Gallister smiled. His brimming self-confidence made the expression a little smarmy. "Surely we can come to some sort of an agreement, Detective Travis. I mean, you're a beautiful young woman. I've always been able to make beautiful young women see that I have only their best interests at heart."

"My best interest is in solving this case," Travis said.

Gallister's smile slipped and then disappeared. "No, your best interest is in avoiding the sort of trouble that's going to come raining down on your head if you don't listen to reason," he snapped. "You have no right to hold this boat and its passengers. I have the largest legal practice in St. Louis on retainer, you know. I'll call my lawyers—"

"If you feel you need to do that, Mr. Gallister, you go right ahead."

"I won't be held hostage by some small-town police department! Just what do you think you're going to accomplish by these high-handed tactics?"

"I plan to question everyone on this boat," Travis said. "I'm also in the process of getting a search warrant so that it can be searched from top to bottom. If there's anything here relating to Ben Webster's murder, we're going to find it."

"Very thorough, I'm sure," Gallister said with a sneer. Charm hadn't worked, and neither had bluster. Now he was trying disdain. "We'll just see what my attorneys have to say about this."

He turned and stomped away like a little kid who had threatened to take his ball and go home only to be told that he couldn't. He could leave if he wanted to, but the ball—or in this case, the riverboat—had to stay where it was.

Williams tried to mend fences with Travis. "I'm sorry, Detective," he said. "I'm sure Mr. Gallister meant no disrespect—"

"Of course not," Travis said dryly. "He's just used to getting his way."

Williams shrugged. "For the record, I think you should allow us to return to St. Louis, too. You know it's inevitable. Mr. Gallister's lawyers will be able to find a judge willing to sign a court order releasing the *Southern Belle* and everyone on it from police custody."

"I'll deal with that when it happens," Travis said. "Now, if you'll excuse me, Captain, I'm going to ask to borrow your salon so that I can question the passengers there. I'll need a copy of your manifest, too. Oh, and I'm shutting down the casino."

Williams looked like he wanted to yelp in protest. His bushy white eyebrows went up as he said, "You can't shut down the casino. Gambling is legal in Missouri, and we're in Missouri waters."

"I consider it a hindrance to a police investigation, so I'm within my rights to close it temporarily. That's something *else* Mr. Gallister's attorneys can take up with their tame judge, I suppose."

Now she was just being spiteful, I thought. But maybe I couldn't blame her. She had a murder investigation to conduct, and she had to be aware of the size of the obstacles a man like Charles Gallister could—and would—throw into her path.

Travis went on, "Will you give the orders, Captain, or shall I?"

Williams sighed. "I'll tell the crew members working in the casino to clear out the passengers and close down. You're going to have a lot of unhappy people on your hands, though."

"Let me worry about that," Travis said. Then she turned toward me, and I knew she was going to want to question me first. Not only was the murdered man one of my clients, but I had mentioned the other murder that had taken place on the *Southern Belle*. That probably had Detective Travis pretty curious.

So naturally, just as Travis started toward me, my phone picked that exact moment to ring.

Travis paused and frowned. I slipped the phone from my pocket and saw that Melissa was calling from the office again. I opened it and said, "Sorry, honey, this still isn't a very good time for me to copy down that serial number from my computer—"

"I'm not calling about that, Mom," Melissa said. "I decided to do some more digging on the computer here about Ben Webster. And I found out something interesting."

I held up one finger toward Detective Travis, asking for a minute of time. I didn't like it much when folks did that to me, and judging by the frown on Travis's face, neither did she. But I wanted to hear what Melissa had to say.

"Go ahead," I told her. "What did you find out?" I avoided saying Webster's name where Travis could overhear what we were talking about.

On the other end of the phone, Melissa didn't have to worry about that. She said, "The only thing I've really found out about Ben Webster, Mom, . . . is that apparently he doesn't exist."

CHAPTER 16

For a second I thought I hadn't heard her correctly. Of course Ben Webster existed. I had talked to him. I had seen him when he was alive, and I had seen him when he was dead. Maybe Melissa was speaking metaphorically. Webster was dead, so he no longer existed. . . .

Nah. I love my daughter and she's smart as a whip, but she isn't the type to sit around the office making philosophical comments. If she said Webster didn't exist, she meant it literally.

"I don't see how that's possible," I said carefully as Detective Travis started to look impatient.

"I checked out the address on the credit card he gave us. It would be in the middle of a lake, if there were such an address. There isn't."

"How's that possible?" I was so bumfuzzled I was starting to sound like a broken record.

"It's a new card. Webster must not have used it for anything else, so he hasn't gotten a bill yet. He must've had some sort of fake ID in order to get the credit card, but those aren't hard to put your hands on these days."

That was certainly true. Identity theft and credit card fraud were booming businesses.

Melissa went on, "Once I found out the address was a phony, I did some more checking. According to the Social Security database, there are dozens of Benjamin Websters around the country who are close to the right age . . . but none in the St. Louis area, which is where our Webster claimed to be from. I did a public records search and didn't find anybody who matches his info, Mom. I think he must have had a phony driver's license and Social Security number. He's somebody else. He's not Ben Webster."

As Melissa had said, that was mighty interesting. I wondered if Detective Travis knew about it yet. I figured the crime scene techs had taken Webster's fingerprints, and Travis had probably submitted them to the national databases available to law enforcement agencies. But from what I'd heard, it sometimes took several days to get a match from those databases, even if one existed. The dead man's real identity might still be a mystery.

Along with who killed him.

Travis was starting to look really annoyed now, so I said into the phone, "I'm glad you let me know about that, but I've got to go right now. I'll call you later."

"Yeah, I still need to give you those numbers for the insurance claim."

"Thanks, sweetheart." I closed the phone and

put it away, saying as I did so, "My daughter. She runs the office for me, back in Atlanta."

"I'm sorry to interfere with your business, Ms. Dickinson," Travis said, but she didn't really sound all that sorry. "Now, if you'll come with me to the salon . . ."

I nodded. I didn't like it much, but ready or not, I was about to be interrogated.

Travis led the way into the salon. She went to the bar, showed her badge to the bartender, and told him, "The salon is going to be closed for a while. You can check with Captain Williams about that if you want to."

"Yes, ma'am, I'll do that," the bartender said, then picked up a phone that probably connected him to the pilothouse. He turned away, spoke in a quiet tone for a couple of minutes, then said, "Yes, sir, I understand."

He hung up, turned back to us, and tossed the bar rag he was holding onto the hardwood. "The place is all yours, Detective."

It was still early enough in the morning that not many people were in the salon, only half a dozen or so. I was sure the casino was busier. The bartender went around the room and told everyone that the salon was closing for the time being. That drew some puzzled looks, but nobody argued with him. The passengers just got up and left.

Travis motioned for me to have a seat at one of the tables. She sat down across from me and took out her notebook. She said, "Tell me everything you can about your contacts with Ben Webster, Ms. Dickinson."

"We went over all that yesterday, didn't we?"

"Humor me," she said. "Tell me again."

I knew she was trying to trip me up, to catch me in a lie. But since I had told her the truth the day before, I didn't have to worry about that. I just told the whole thing to her again, up to and including the fact that I'd fainted when Logan Rafferty and Captain Williams showed me Webster's body.

I was hoping she had forgotten about what I'd blurted out earlier, but no such luck. When I was finished going over my story, she said, "A while ago you mentioned another unsolved murder that took place here on the *Southern Belle*. What do you know about that?"

"Not much, just that a young woman was killed here last year."

"A year ago today, to be precise," Travis said. "Doesn't that strike you as odd, Ms. Dickinson?"

"Well, sure. But coincidences happen, even gruesome ones like this one."

"You're certain it's a coincidence?"

"I don't know of any connection between the woman who was killed last year and Ben Webster."

But I didn't know who Ben Webster really was, I reminded myself. I suddenly realized that he could have known Hannah Kramer. It was even possible that he was the person who had *killed* Hannah Kramer.

That thought made a chill go through me. Louise had mentioned that Hannah met a man in St. Louis. That man could have been Webster.

They could have broken up, and he could have followed her onto the boat and . . .

But why take the same cruise a year later? Maybe he was a serial killer, I thought. Maybe it was some sort of ritual for him. Take a riverboat cruise, kill another passenger.

Webster was the one who was dead, though. He was the victim. I was letting my brain run away with itself and fill itself with crazy theories.

Theories that I couldn't actually disprove, crazy or not.

Detective Travis was saying, "What *do* you know about the woman who was killed last year?"

I could plead ignorance and claim that I'd just heard some vague rumors. But then if Travis questioned Louise Kramer, and Louise testified that she had told me all about the facts of the case, then I might look pretty bad in Travis's eyes. Plus, by nature I'm just not the sort to lie to the police unless there's a mighty good reason for doing so.

"I know her name was Hannah Kramer," I said. "Her parents are on this cruise."

That ruffled Detective Travis's previously unflappable demeanor. She said, "They are?"

I nodded. "Yes. They came on it as a sort of . . . farewell to their daughter, I guess you'd say."

"That's just morbid."

Travis's display of distaste was one of the first signs of true emotion I'd seen from her. I said, "Oh, I don't know. Folks grieve in different ways, I guess."

"Did you know about this before the cruise started?"

I shook my head. "No, not at all. Eddie and Louise Kramer were just names to me, and I'd never even heard of Hannah."

"I had," Travis said. "I remember when it happened. I was still working patrol. I hadn't been promoted to detective yet."

"I know it happened while the boat was moving, which meant it was during the day. I'm surprised nobody saw anything."

It was Travis's turn to shake her head. "No, the *Southern Belle* had a dinner cruise then. The boat still docked at Hannibal during the afternoon, but that evening it cruised up and down the river so the passengers could dine outside on the deck. It never went very far, just a mile or two upriver and then back down."

"Sounds romantic."

Travis shrugged. "Not for Hannah Kramer. But that's why it was dark when she was killed." She frowned at me. "I'm supposed to be the one asking questions here."

I shrugged. "Just talkin', Detective. But that ought to prove to you that I didn't know anything about that other case."

"Unless that's what you wanted me to think."

I held up my hands. "Hey, I'd never been on this boat before yesterday. And a year ago I was in Atlanta."

"I suppose you can prove that."

I thought back for a second, then said, "As a matter of fact, I can. I was in court a year ago on this date."

"Court?" Travis asked as she raised her eyebrows.

"Getting divorced. I reckon you can get all kinds of documentation about that."

"I don't think I need it," she said with another shake of her head. "But it's nice to know it exists if I do." She looked at her notebook, but I wasn't convinced she was actually checking anything. I think it was just a habit, or to make me think she was looking at something. "Tell me more about the Kramers. Have you gotten to know them during the cruise?"

"Well, sure, a little," I said with a shrug. "Louise more so than her husband."

"He seems a little loud."

I didn't know what she was trying to get me to say. Maybe she knew about the cell phone incident the day before, early in the cruise, or the confrontation in the dining room. So I said, "Mr. Kramer's got a lot on his mind, especially right now, I imagine."

"Do you know of any connection between them and Ben Webster? Did you see either of them talking to him yesterday?"

I was able to answer that with an honest, "No, I sure didn't. As far as I know, they weren't acquainted with Mr. Webster at all."

"As far as you know."

"That's all I can tell you," I said. "I can't tell you what I don't know."

"No, of course not," Travis agreed. "What about Mark Lansing?"

That quick change of subject was an interrogation technique. I knew that from TV—and from being mixed up in a murder investigation the year before. I didn't let it throw me. I said, "You probably already know that Mr. Lansing and I have spent some time together since yesterday. I'd say we're friends, even though we haven't known each other very long."

"Do you know him well enough to be aware that he's a private detective?"

If she was trying to surprise something out of me, it didn't work this time, either. I nodded and said, "Yes, I did." I didn't go into detail about how I'd found out that fact. I wasn't surprised that Travis knew about Mark's real job. She had probably run the names of everyone on the boat through the computer, and it would have spit out the fact that Mark was a licensed private detective.

Like a bulldog, Travis didn't let go. "Did he tell you, or did you find out some other way?"

I didn't want to get tangled up in lies, so I figured it would be best to continue telling the truth. "He didn't tell me. Someone else did."

"And who was that?"

I hesitated. "Isn't there some sort of right to confidentiality between private eyes and their clients?"

"A private investigator working for an attorney is sometimes protected by attorney-client privilege." Travis smiled and shook her head. "But I'm afraid there's not any sort of travel agent–client privilege."

She had me boxed in. I sighed and said, "Mark was hired by Louise Kramer. She told me about it. She thinks that someone who worked on the riverboat last year was responsible for Hannah's murder, and that whomever it was might still be working here. She's known Mark since they were both kids. She thought maybe he could find out something."

"Something that the police haven't been able to find, you mean."

I shrugged. "The case is still open."

"Which means that a private detective shouldn't be involved with it."

"That's between him and the police."

"Did Mrs. Kramer tell you if he'd found out anything yet?"

"No, she didn't." I was getting tired of this.

Maybe Detective Travis sensed that, because she said, "I think that's all for now, Ms. Dickinson. Thank you for your cooperation."

I just nodded. I wasn't going to say that it wasn't a problem, or anything like that, because it was. I would answer her questions, but I didn't have to like it.

As I stood up, I asked, "We're all still confined to the boat?"

"For the time being," Travis answered without looking up.

I left the salon. I didn't know whom she was going to question next, but that was her business, not mine. I headed up to the third deck, instead. The chain that closed off the deck along the crew quarters was down at the moment, so I didn't have to unhook it. I was able to march right down the deck to Mark's cabin and knock on the door.

Lo and behold, he was actually there this

time. He looked surprised to see me when he opened the door. But he smiled like he was glad I was there.

"Hi, Delilah. I was hoping you'd stop by. Have you heard anything about whether or not we'll be able to get off the boat anytime soon?"

"The detective in charge of the case is bein' hard-nosed about keeping us on board while she questions everybody," I told him.

"That's going to take a while," he said with a frown. "Between the passengers and the crew, there are quite a few people on this boat."

"Yeah, that's right," I said. "Even if you eliminate the passengers, that's still a lot of murder suspects."

Mark's frown deepened. "Why would you eliminate the passengers? I'm not sure anybody who works on the *Southern Belle* would have had a reason to kill Ben Webster."

I still had my suspicions about Logan Rafferty, not to mention the fella Webster had accused of cheating in the casino. But I didn't bring that up now. Instead, I said, "I'm not talkin' about Ben Webster. I'm talkin' about whoever killed Hannah Kramer."

CHAPTER 17

I had finally succeeded in taking him completely by surprise. His jaw practically dropped. He was too much in control of his emotions to let his reaction go quite that far, though. It didn't last long, either. A second after the words were out of my mouth, his face was once again carefully expressionless.

"I'm afraid I don't know what you're talking about," he said.

I put a hand in the middle of his chest and pushed him backward into his room. Of course, he was a lot bigger than me and I probably couldn't have budged him if he hadn't let me, but he didn't put up a fight. He probably wanted to find out just how much I actually knew.

"Forget it," I told him as I closed the door behind me. "Louise Kramer told me the whole thing. I know about her daughter and about the two of you bein' old friends. I even know that you're a private eye." I crossed my arms over my chest and glared at him. "Let me tell you, that's better than what I was thinkin' when Louise tried to sneak into your cabin last night and then I saw her comin' out of here earlier and you hugged her like the two of you had just climbed out of the sack."

"Delilah!"

"Oh, don't act so shocked. Aren't all private eyes sophisticated men of the world?"

Mark shook his head. "You've got it all wrong. There's nothing going on between Louise and me."

"Didn't I just say that? I know that y'all are just friends. And that she's your client."

"You say that she came here last night? You saw her and talked to her then? Why didn't you say anything?"

"No, I didn't talk to her. Until this morning, I didn't know who the woman was who let herself into your cabin with a key and called your name in the wee hours of the mornin'. What the heck was I supposed to think?"

He looked confused. After a second he said, "If I had a girlfriend coming to my cabin last night, would I have offered the place to you like I did?"

I narrowed my eyes at him. "Maybe you had some serious foolin' around in mind."

He held up his hands, palms out, and said, "Delilah, I swear—"

"Oh, relax," I told him. "I know now what's goin' on, remember? Louise explained the whole thing to me. I'm not mad at you for havin' a girl-friend." I snorted. Unladylike, I know, but that was the only way to express what I was feeling just then. "Anyway, even if you had a girlfriend, it wouldn't be any of my business, now would it?"

He didn't answer that. Instead he asked, "What did Louise tell you?"

I laid it all out for him, just like she had with me in the dining room. Somehow while we were talking, we wound up sitting down, me in the room's only chair, Mark on the edge of the bed. When I was finished telling him what Louise had told me, I said, "What about it? Have you found out anything about Hannah Kramer's murder?"

The question made him look uncomfortable. "That's really between me and my client, isn't it?"

"It would be if Detective Travis wasn't trying to find some connection between Hannah's murder and what happened to Ben Webster yesterday."

"But there's not any connection," Mark said. He rubbed his jaw in thought. "I've looked into the time that Hannah lived in St. Louis, after she left Kennett. She didn't know anybody named Webster there."

"You've found out the names of everybody she knew?"

"Well, no, I suppose not. That would be pretty difficult. People have lots of acquaintances who don't play any major part in their lives."

"Louise said that Hannah got involved with a man in St. Louis. Do you know his name?"

Mark frowned. "I haven't been able to find out who he was yet. She didn't really confide in her neighbors in the apartment house or any-thing like that."

"So you don't know. She might have been dating Ben Webster. She could have dumped him, and he could have come on the riverboat to either win her back . . . or kill her."

Except for the fact that Ben Webster wasn't really his name, I reminded myself. The dead man's true identity was still a mystery. So even if Mark had been able to find out who Hannah's boyfriend was, he probably wouldn't have been going by Ben Webster.

"That doesn't make sense," Mark said. "Webster's dead, too. If he killed Hannah—and I think that's really unlikely—then who killed him?"

Eddie Kramer, maybe, I thought. But if Mark didn't know whether or not Webster had been Hannah's boyfriend, then how in the heck could Eddie have found out?

My head was starting to hurt from trying to keep up with all this.

I had something to trade, I told myself. I might not know who the latest murder victim really was, but I knew who he wasn't. Maybe that was tied in with the case Mark was working on. Maybe it wasn't. But the best way to start finding out was for both of us to lay our cards on the table.

"Why don't you tell me everything you've been able to find out about Hannah?" I suggested. "And I'll tell you what I know about Ben Webster."

"Webster's got nothing to do with this."

"How do you *know* that?"

He thought about that for a second, then slowly nodded. "All right. You've got a point there. But you probably know most of this already."

"Tell me anyway," I said, realizing that I was starting to sound like Detective Travis. Maybe if the literary tour business went bust, I could start a new career as a cop.

That was a laugh.

"Louise told you that her mom and my mom are best friends, I imagine."

I nodded. "She did."

"If you ever lived in a small town, you know how strong the grapevine is. Everybody keeps up with everybody else's business, even when somebody moves away. So Louise knew that I was a detective."

"Not a lawyer," I said with an accusatory tone in my voice.

Mark spread his hands and gave me a rueful smile. "I know, I lied to you. I'm sorry. I'm working undercover, though. You can't expect me to just blurt out who I really am and what I'm doing to everybody I meet . . . even really good-looking redheads."

"Flattery's not necessary. Don't think that means I don't appreciate it, but it's not necessary."

"I actually do a lot of work for various law firms, so while I may not be a lawyer, I work for them most of the time. I don't take on many cases for individual clients like Louise. I wouldn't have taken this one if she hadn't been an old friend."

"Why not?"

"A murder that's a year old?" He shook his head. "That's a pretty cold case. Plus, when you start digging around in people's lives, you never know what you're going to find out. I might have uncovered something about Hannah that Louise would have rather not known. I still might."

"Like who her boyfriend in St. Louis was?"

"Yeah." He paused. "Or who the father of her child was, if it's not the same guy."

I couldn't help but stare at him. "Child?" I repeated.

"Yeah. Hannah Kramer was pregnant when she died."

That was a shocker, although in this day and age, when it seems like more unmarried women are pregnant than the ones with wedding rings on their fingers, I don't know why it should have been.

"Did her folks know about that?"

"Sure. The autopsy turned up the fact that she was three months pregnant, and of course the police questioned Louise and Eddie about it. They wanted to know who the father was, since he'd automatically be a suspect in the murder, at least until it was established whether or not he had an alibi. But Louise and Eddie didn't know anything about it, except that Hannah had been seeing somebody. And Louise was the only one who actually knew that. Hannah and her father didn't talk much after the big blowup they had that resulted in her moving away from home."

"Nobody who knew Hannah in St. Louis had any idea?"

"Evidently she kept pretty much to herself," Mark said. "She was a shy girl. Not really the sort to work as a cocktail waitress in a riverboat casino, although she was pretty enough to do so. Nobody here on board the *Southern Belle* had any complaints about her work, other than the fact that she was sick fairly often."

"Morning sickness," I said.

"Yeah, that's my guess."

Hannah's pregnancy added another whole layer to the mystery of her death. Not only was the identity of the baby's father unknown, but so was whether or not the pregnancy had any connection to her death.

A picture was starting to form in my mind. It was fuzzy, but still a picture. If Ben Webster had been Hannah's boyfriend, if he was the father of her baby, he could have come on board the riverboat now in an attempt to track down her killer and avenge her death. While it was unlikely he would be able to solve her murder in less than a day when the police had been unsuccessful for a whole year, that possibility couldn't be ruled out. Maybe Webster figured out who the killer was, confronted him, and then whoever it was had committed a second murder to keep from being exposed. As far as I could see, the theory hung together—but it was just a theory, with lots of blank spaces in it where information still needed to be filled in.

I looked at Mark and wondered if the same idea had occurred to him. I had to ask myself if

I trusted him enough to share it with him. He had come clean with me, but only when I had already found out most of what was going on myself and he'd been forced to.

He didn't know about Webster not being Webster, either. I had promised him I'd be honest with him if he was honest with me, so I didn't see any way out of telling him what I knew.

Before I did, though, there were still a couple of things I wanted to know from him. "What have you been doing since I saw Louise come out of your cabin earlier? I looked around the boat for you but couldn't find you."

"I was down below decks talking to some of the engine room crew. They wouldn't have had that much to do with Hannah while she was working on the boat, but I'm running out of people to ask about her."

"Don't they wonder why the guy who plays Mark Twain is asking so many questions?"

"Please," Mark said. "I don't just come right out and say, 'Remember that girl who was murdered last year? Who do you think might have killed her?' Give me credit for a little more subtlety than that."

"Did you find out anything?"

He shook his head. "Not a blasted thing. Actually, all they wanted to talk about was Ben Webster's murder."

"They have any ideas about that?"

"I'm afraid not. Henry, the guy who found the body, is still pretty shaken up about it."

"That corridor where the storage locker is . . .

it doesn't have a security camera covering it, does it?"

Mark laughed, but there was no humor in the sound. "The cops can't be that lucky. There's no camera. The killer wasn't caught on tape stuffing Webster's body into the locker."

"Is that corridor used very much?"

"Actually, no. It's not the main access to the engine room. Nothing's down there but the little closet where Webster's body was found and some hatches that give access to the pipes running between the boilers and the engine room."

"You think whoever hid Webster's body there knew that?" I asked. "Seems to me that if they did, they must know a lot about the boat and how it operates."

He nodded slowly. "That's a good thought. Somebody could have carried the body down there on the spur of the moment and stashed it the first place they came to—"

"But it's more likely they went down there with Webster and killed him right then and there," I said, even as the conclusion formed in my mind.

"Yeah," Mark said. "That would be a lot less risky than hauling a corpse down from one of the upper decks."

"That would mean it's pretty likely Webster knew his killer, and maybe even trusted him," I pointed out.

Mark shrugged. "Or had some other good reason to go with him, like a gun in his back."

"Forcing Webster below decks at gunpoint

seems almost as risky to me as killing him up above and then carryin' him down."

"That's true," Mark admitted. "This is interesting speculation, Delilah, but that's all it is. And it doesn't have anything to do with Hannah Kramer's murder, at least as far as we know now."

"Maybe," I said with a note of stubbornness in my voice. "I know coincidences exist in this world, but it seems like a real stretch to me to think that two people could be killed on the same riverboat, almost exactly a year apart, and the two cases not have *some* connection."

He grinned. "Maybe you should be a private detective."

I snorted again. "No, thank you. I'm perfectly happy doin' what I'm doin'. . . . At least I am when nobody gets themselves murdered on one of my tours!"

CHAPTER 18

Mark had told me all he knew, or at least he claimed he had. All I could do was take his word for it. But I didn't think he was lying, so I knew it was time for me to keep my part of the bargain.

"Even though we don't know for sure that Ben Webster's murder is connected to Hannah's," I said, "I found out something about Webster that might interest you."

"I'm all ears," he said.

Actually, his ears weren't abnormally big. They were just the right size for his head. But I pushed that distracting thought out of my brain and went on, "My daughter, Melissa, did some diggin' around on the computer about Webster, and she discovered that he was usin' a phony name."

Mark frowned in surprise and asked, "He wasn't really Ben Webster?"

"Nope. The credit card he used to pay for this trip was legit, but the billing address on it doesn't exist. The info he gave us doesn't match up with any of the Ben Websters in the Social Security database, either. It was a false identity, or a stolen one."

Mark rubbed his jaw again as he thought over what I'd just told him. "Then he must have been some sort of criminal," he said slowly.

"You'd think so." Another possibility occurred to me. "Either that, or he was hiding out from somebody."

"And they caught up to him and killed him?"

I shrugged. "That would explain the murder. *That* murder, anyway. I don't see how it ties in with Hannah's."

Mark smiled. "After you think about all the possibilities for a while, it makes you want to tear your hair out, doesn't it?"

"My head already hurts bad enough without tearin' any hair out."

We likely would have hashed things out some more—and probably not reached any conclusions—but right then Mark's cell phone rang. He took it out of his pocket, looked at the display, and frowned.

"Winston, Pine, and Blevins," he said. "That's a law firm in St. Louis I do most of my work for. I guess I'd better take this."

"Go ahead," I told him.

He opened the phone, said, "Hello." With a frown of concentration on his face, he listened for a minute, then said, "That's a very appealing offer, Mr. Pine, but I'm already involved in a case right now . . . How much? . . . And the client asked for me in particular? . . . How did they know? . . . I see. When do you need an answer?" His mouth tightened. "I don't see how I can . . . Yes, sir, I understand . . . I'm sorry. I just can't do it." He took a deep breath. "Of course. Good-bye."

Then he looked at me as he closed the phone and added, "Well, that sucks."

"What happened?"

"One of the firm's biggest clients wanted them to hire me to do some investigative work. And the job would start immediately, as in today, as soon as I could get back to St. Louis."

"How come you didn't tell them you're stuck in Hannibal until Detective Travis decides to let us go?"

Mark shook his head. "It wouldn't matter. Even if we weren't being held here, I gave Louise my word. I can't just drop one case to take on another one, no matter how lucrative it might be . . . or how detrimental it's going to be to turn down the job."

"What do you mean by that?"

"Mr. Pine—the partner I was talking to—made it clear that if I didn't accept the offer, I wouldn't be getting any more assignments from Winston, Pine, and Blevins in the future." He shrugged. "And like I said, I did more work for them than any other law firm."

"That's terrible," I said. "And not fair at all."

He shrugged. "Nobody ever said life was fair, now did they?"

"If they did, they were dead wrong," I agreed. "Still, this just isn't right."

More than that, I found it odd. Something

stirred in the back of my mind, but I couldn't drag it far enough into the light to make out what it was. All I could sense was a connection I wasn't quite seeing.

"Right or not," Mark said, "I'll stick with Louise's case. If she doesn't find out what happened to Hannah, it's going to haunt her for the rest of her life. And that *really* wouldn't be fair."

"You're right. What do we do now?"

He raised his eyebrows. "We?"

"Consider me your assistant," I said. "Watson to your Holmes."

Mark laughed. "You're giving me *way* too much credit for my deductive abilities. I'm a plodder, not an eccentric genius. Besides, I play Mark Twain, not Sherlock Holmes, remember?"

"Well, Twain wrote a book called *Tom Sawyer, Detective*, didn't he?"

"He did," Mark admitted with a shrug.

"If it's good enough for Tom Sawyer, it's good enough for us. I'll be Becky Thatcher."

He laughed again. "I'm not sure she's in that book, but all right. I can see you're not going to give up. What do we do next?"

"I can't shake the feeling that there might be a connection between Hannah's murder and what happened to the fella callin' himself Ben Webster. Have you been on board long enough to know who runs the roulette wheel in the casino?"

"As a matter of fact, I have."

"Let's go see if we can find him and have a talk with him," I said.

* * *

With the casino closed, all the people who normally worked there didn't have anything to do. And with the salon being used by Detective Travis to conduct her questioning of everybody on the *Southern Belle*, the crew members couldn't go there to drink. Mark had heard rumors, though, that there was a party going on below decks for the duration of the riverboat's enforced stay in Hannibal.

We headed down the four flights of stairs that took us to the boat's lower level. There was a mess hall for the crew down there, Mark explained, so the people who worked on the *Southern Belle* didn't have to eat in the same dining room as the passengers. We heard the sound of talk and laughter before we even got there.

When we reached the mess hall, we found it crowded. Even though the sun wasn't anywhere near the yardarm, to use a nautical term that didn't have anything to do with riverboats, I saw quite a bit of drinking going on, as well as a poker game where a couple of tables had been pushed together. I wondered what poker was like for a bunch of professional dealers. Sort of a busman's holiday, I expected, but what else did they have to do while they were stuck here?

Several people greeted Mark with reserved smiles. He was the new guy on board, after all. They glanced somewhat suspiciously at me. I was a passenger. To their way of thinking, I didn't belong down here.

But as the leader of a tour group, I wasn't a

regular passenger. It could be argued that I worked on the *Southern Belle*, the same as the rest of the folks gathered in this mess hall did.

As we crossed the room, I could tell that there was a considerable amount of flirting going on among the crew, too. You throw a bunch of men and women together in a work environment and there are bound to be some romances, no matter how many rules there are against them. Some things you just can't legislate or regulate, and the effect of hormones is one of 'em. Don't let anybody tell you it only happens among younger folks, either. Listen to the gossip in retirement homes, if you don't believe me.

That might have something to do with Hannah Kramer's murder, I told myself. She could have gotten involved with someone who worked on the riverboat, and her death could have been the result of a lover's quarrel.

But that wasn't true of Ben Webster. He had been on board for only a few hours before he was killed. He hadn't had time to start any sort of romance with either another passenger or a member of the crew. And we were here to poke into Webster's murder right now, in hopes that investigating it might lead to something that would have a bearing on Hannah's death, too.

Mark led me to a table in the corner where a man sat alone. "Hello, Garvey," he said. "You know Delilah Dickinson, don't you?"

The man wore a sullen expression on his face as he shook his head. He had a half-empty beer bottle on the table in front of him, the fingers of one hand wrapped loosely around it.

"Can't say as I do," he said. "One of the passengers, isn't she?"

I thought that was sort of rude, talking about me like I wasn't even there. So I said, "No, not exactly. I'm the leader of one of the tour groups."

The man called Garvey grunted. "Same thing."

I felt a surge of anger but didn't show it. "No, this is my job," I said with a smile. "I work on the boat, just like you do. Mind if we sit down?"

He nodded toward the empty chairs at the table. "Help yourselves."

We sat down, and Mark said, "This is a pretty rotten deal, isn't it, being stuck here like this? I don't know about you, but I need to get back to St. Louis."

Garvey shrugged. "It doesn't matter all that much to me. I don't have any family there. And I get paid either way, whether we're steaming back down the river or not."

"Yeah, but I don't like the way the cops are questioning everybody, like we're suspects or something," Mark said.

"Huh," Garvey said. "You don't have anything to worry about. I'm the one who had trouble yesterday with that son of a bitch who got killed." He glanced at me. "No offense. I know he was one of your clients."

I leaned forward over the table and said, "Did that lady cop question you already? She was all over me earlier, just because Webster was a member of my tour. I never even saw the guy before lunch yesterday! Why would I have any reason to kill him?"

"Of course you wouldn't," Garvey agreed. "He didn't take a swing at you." He drank from his beer and added hastily, "Don't take that to mean I had anything to do with what happened to him. I was working in the casino all afternoon yesterday and never left it. I've got witnesses to prove that, and that's what I told that cop." A humorless chuckle came from him. "Anyway, it's not like that was the first time anybody ever accused me of running a crooked wheel. Hell, I ought to be used to it by now. I've had customers threaten me before."

"Really?" Mark said.

"You've always got sore losers to deal with. That's just part of the job." A cynical grin appeared on Garvey's narrow face. "Of course, there might be a few more than usual on the *Southern Belle.*"

Before either of us could ask him what he meant by that, a large presence loomed up beside us. I turned my head to see Logan Rafferty standing there. "What are you going on about now, Clyde?" he asked Garvey.

"Nothing, Mr. Rafferty, nothing," Garvey said. He almost tripped over the words, and I could tell he was nervous. Rafferty had that effect on people, especially when he was towering over them like a mountain about to come crashing down on them.

Rafferty looked at me and frowned. "What

are you doing here, Ms. Dickinson? Not that you're not welcome, but this is a crew area. It's normally off limits to passengers."

"I brought her with me," Mark said. "I figured Delilah's not exactly the same as a regular passenger, since being on the boat is part of her job, just like it is with ours."

Rafferty's massive shoulders rose and fell in a shrug. "I suppose you could look at it that way," he said. "I wouldn't go wandering around by yourself in places you're not supposed to be, though, Ms. Dickinson."

"I don't intend to," I told him. "And I can go back up on deck right now if you want."

He waved a big hand. "No, no, that's all right. You're welcome down here." He turned back to Garvey. "I need to have a word with you in private, Clyde."

A small, nervous tic in Garvey's jaw increased in its frequency. But he nodded and said, "All right, sure."

"Let's go up to my office," Rafferty suggested as Garvey stood up.

Garvey looked a little like a man being marched to the gallows as he left the mess hall with Rafferty. When they were gone, Mark leaned toward me and asked in a quiet voice, "What do you think that was all about?"

"This is just a guess," I said, "but I'll bet Rafferty wants to find out what Detective Travis asked Garvey about that trouble with Ben Webster yesterday . . . and what Garvey told her."

Mark nodded as he thought about it, then said, "You know, from the way Garvey was talking, it's not unusual for people to complain about the roulette wheel. Do you think that's because it really is rigged?"

"You mean Webster was right about bein' cheated?" I shook my head. "I don't know. I'd think that the boat makes plenty of money without riggin' the games, but short of takin' a look at the books, I don't know how we'd ever prove that."

"For some people, there's no such thing as plenty of money," Mark pointed out. "They always want more and more, no matter how much they've got."

"That's true." I thought about it, then said, "And just because the *boat* makes money, that doesn't mean everything in the casino is on the up-and-up. The profits from the *Southern Belle* go in Charles Gallister's pocket. Maybe if there's something funny going on in the casino, it's somebody else's operation."

"Like Logan Rafferty's?"

We looked at each other and shook our heads at the same time. "We're jumping to way too many conclusions," Mark went on.

"Maybe, but that doesn't necessarily mean we're wrong," I pointed out. "It's something to think about."

Instinctively, I had disliked and distrusted Logan Rafferty from the moment I met him. I could easily see him setting up some sort of crooked scheme in the casino involving a rigged roulette wheel. Maybe after giving me the slip the day before, Ben Webster had continued poking around until he found the proof he needed to show everybody that he'd been right about being cheated. If Rafferty was behind it, then he'd have had a good reason to break Webster's neck.

But it seemed like everywhere I looked, there was *somebody* with a potential good reason—or more than one—to have broken Webster's neck. Except across the table, of course. Mark had come on board the *Southern Belle* with secrets of his own, no doubt about that, but none of them had anything to do with Ben Webster.

"The casino is closed for the time bein'," I said, "but that doesn't mean you couldn't get in there if you wanted to, does it?"

"Do I want to?" Mark asked with a grin.

"I don't know about you," I said, "but I'd sort of like to take a look at that roulette wheel of Garvey's."

"Do you know what you'd be looking for? No offense, Delilah, but since when are you an expert on rigged roulette wheels?"

"I'm not," I admitted. "I'm just hopin' that it's like pornography."

That comment brought a puzzled frown to Mark's face.

"I'll know it when I see it," I said.

CHAPTER 19

The casino had two main entrances from the deck, one on the port side, one on the starboard. Detective Travis had posted a uniformed officer at each door to keep everybody out.

She must not have known about the little passage linking the kitchen adjacent to the dining room with the bar in the casino as well. People went to the casino to gamble, not to eat, but many of them drank while they were there and sometimes passengers in the dining room wanted a beer or a glass of wine or a cocktail with their meals. So it made sense to connect things behind the scenes.

That's what Mark and I were trying to do, I thought as we made our way through the kitchen and into the narrow hallway behind the casino, ignoring the curious looks that the kitchen staff gave us as they prepared lunch. If we could connect enough apparently unrelated things, we might come up with a picture that started to make sense.

We weren't there yet, though. I hoped that examining the roulette wheel would give us some more information.

The little door behind the bar in the casino wasn't locked. Mark opened it, and we stepped into the large, shadowy room. The slot machines were still plugged in and lit up. They provided the only illumination inside the casino, but that was enough for us to be able to see our way around.

We headed straight for the roulette wheel, which stood silent and motionless without a human hand to launch it into action. Even though no one else was in here, I whispered as I told Mark, "Webster said the man operating the machine—that'd be Clyde Garvey, I guess— kept touching one particular spot on it, like there was a switch of some sort there."

"It couldn't be anything that was too visible," Mark whispered back. "But if there was a place on the machine where the wood was thinner, it might be flexible enough so that you could depress it and activate a pressure switch hidden underneath it."

"How do we go about findin' it?"

"I don't suppose Webster told you exactly where the place was that Garvey kept fiddling with?"

"No such luck," I said.

"Then we'll just have to check it over as best we can. I'll take this side, and you take that one. Run your fingers over it and feel for any soft spots."

"Like the soft spot on a baby's head?"

Mark smiled in the gloom. "I've never been around kids all that much, but yeah, I guess so. Not quite that soft, though."

"You never had any kids of your own?"

"I never got married . . . much to my mom's dismay."

I started sliding my fingers over the smooth wood of the table on which the roulette wheel was mounted. "You don't have to be married to have kids," I pointed out. "Hannah Kramer was proof of that."

"Yeah, well, I'm just old-fashioned enough that it seems like a good idea to me for one to come before the other. I like doing things in the proper order." He searched along the other side of the table as he spoke, spreading his fingers and pressing down with them, then moving his hand slightly and trying again when he didn't find anything.

I had been inside the casino while all the games were running, including this wheel. I tried to remember exactly where the operator had stood, figuring that the switch, if there was one, had to be pretty handy to that location. I couldn't recall, though. I hadn't been paying that much attention. A fella could stand almost anywhere around the table to spin the wheel.

After a few minutes, I whispered, "Any luck?"

"Not yet," Mark replied. "Maybe we had the wrong idea about this."

At just that moment, though, I pressed down on the smooth, polished wood of the table and felt it give just slightly under the middle finger of my right hand. I moved my index finger over to that same spot and pressed again, harder this time. The wood definitely flexed, as if it was thinner there than in the surrounding area.

"Mark," I said, "I may have found something."

He hurried around the table. "Where?"

"Right there," I told him, indicating the spot with my fingertip. "You want to try it?"

I slid my finger aside. Mark rested his finger on the wood. It was difficult to be sure in the bad light, but I thought the spot was just a little darker than the surrounding wood. The oil in the skin of the wheel operator's finger had probably caused that, I thought, as it pushed against the hidden switch hundreds, or maybe even thousands, of times.

If there *was* a hidden switch, I reminded myself. "What do you think?" I asked Mark. "Can you feel it?"

He pushed down on the table, leaned close to it and cocked his head so that he could listen. He pressed the spot two or three times, then straightened and grinned at me.

"I can feel the switch engaging, and I can hear it, too," he said. "Webster was right. This wheel is rigged."

"Clyde Garvey must know about it."

"Sure he knows about it," Mark said. "He'd have to, because he's the only one who could activate the switch. I haven't known him very long, but I don't think he would come up with something like this by himself."

"Rafferty," I said.

Mark shrugged. "Could be." He was about to say something else when I sensed as much as saw his muscles stiffening. He leaned closer to me and whispered, "Someone's coming."

I looked at the main doors, but neither of them was opening. Instead, Mark gripped my arm and pointed to the door behind the bar where we had come in. It was swinging open slowly and soundlessly. I hadn't heard the knob turn.

Somebody else had come skulking around.

Mark tugged me away from the roulette wheel. We didn't want to get caught in here, but we couldn't hide behind the bar. That was where the door was opening. We headed for a bank of slot machines instead and ducked behind them. By looking between a couple of the one-armed bandits, we could still see the roulette wheel, but unless whoever was sneaking into the casino knew we were there, they weren't very likely to spot us where we were hidden.

A shadowy figure came out from behind the bar and started across the casino. I could see the person well enough to know that it was a man, and a fairly good-sized one, at that. But not as big as Rafferty, who had been my first thought. I couldn't make out the newcomer's face. When he reached the roulette wheel, he turned so that his back was toward us as he began running his hands along and underneath the table.

Son of a gun, I thought. Whoever he was, he was looking for the same thing Mark and I had been looking for.

But it didn't take him even a minute to find it. I could tell he was pushing with a finger against the same spot where the hidden switch was located. He even bent over to listen and cocked his head, just like Mark. When he straightened, even though he was alone, he gave a nod of satisfaction.

Then he turned so that the glow from the slot machines reached his face, and I had to catch my lower lip between my teeth to keep from gasping in surprise.

The other fella sneaking around the casino was Vince Mallory.

That wasn't the end of the surprises, though. Vince stood there and looked around the darkened casino for a moment, then said, "I know you and Mr. Lansing are in here somewhere, Ms. Dickinson. You might as well come out."

Mark and I looked at each other. Whoever Vince Mallory really was, it was a pretty good bet he wasn't just a former soldier and potential grad student indulging an interest in Mark Twain. I found myself wondering if he really worked for Rafferty.

That didn't make a whole lot of sense, though, I realized. If Vince had been part of the crooked gambling operation, he wouldn't have had to look for the concealed switch on the roulette wheel. He would have known where it was.

I could tell that Mark didn't want to come out of hiding just yet, though, and neither did I. Not until I knew who Vince Mallory really was and knew I could trust him.

Vince sighed and reached inside the back pocket of his jeans. He brought out a wallet, opened it, and held it up, turning so that what was inside the wallet was visible to anyone who was hiding in the casino—like me and Mark.

It was a badge.

"My name really is Vince Mallory, Ms. Dickinson," he said. "I'm a special investigator for the state attorney general's office. I'd appreciate it if you'd cooperate with me."

Mark winced. "I guess we've got to take a chance," he whispered.

"You don't happen to have that gun on you, do you?" I whispered back. "Just in case he's lyin' to us?"

Mark shook his head. "We'll have to risk it. You stay down until I've talked to him."

"No, we'll both get up," I said, letting my stubborn streak come out. Before Mark could argue with me, I put a hand against one of the slot machines to steady myself and rose to my feet, saying, "We're over here, Vince."

He turned toward us with a smooth, unhurried efficiency and smiled as Mark stood up beside me. "I saw the two of you slip into the kitchen and figured you were heading back here," he said as he closed the wallet and put it back in his pocket.

"You knew about the passage between the kitchen and the casino?" Mark asked.

Vince nodded. "I studied the plans of this boat before I ever came aboard, so I'd know my way around. I believe in being prepared when I'm on an assignment."

"You're here to find out if the games are really rigged," I said as understanding dawned on me.

"That's right. There have been quite a few complaints about the gambling on the *Southern Belle*, and we take them seriously. Charles Gallister's an important man, so the AG decided to keep the investigation as quiet as possible until we know more about what we're dealing with." Vince gestured toward the roulette wheel. "And now we know. That wheel, anyway, is as crooked as a dog's hind leg. I'm betting a lot of the other games in here are, too."

"A man as rich as Gallister is supposed to be wouldn't bother with something like that," I said. "If you ask me, somebody else is behind it."

"That's possible," Vince admitted with a shrug. "You're thinking about Logan Rafferty, aren't you?"

"I don't like the son of a gun, I don't mind admittin' that. Cheatin' folks seems like something he'd do."

"Well, now that we have proof that cheating is going on, we'll get to the bottom of it," Vince promised. "Of course, nothing I've found so far is actually admissible as evidence, but once I call the AG's office and get a search warrant, we'll have the State Police swarming all over this boat in a hurry. Rafferty, or whoever's behind the crooked gambling, won't have a chance to cover it up."

"I'll bet you this has got something to do with Ben Webster's murder," I said.

"I'm not here to solve a murder," Vince said with a shrug. "But if Rafferty or someone else involved with this scheme was responsible for Webster's death, it'll all come out in the end. I think you can count on that." He looked at me with a stern expression. "So the two of you can stop playing detective now. I've got this."

Mark opened his mouth to say something, and from the look on his face, the words were going to be angry ones.

Before any of them could come out, I took hold of his arm and squeezed it, hoping he'd understand that I meant for him not to say anything just yet. I spoke up instead. "I guess you're right, Vince. It just bothered the heck out of me that one of my clients was murdered, right in the middle of a tour I'd put together. The only thing I could think of that might have anything to do with what happened to Ben Webster was that ruckus he got into with the fella runnin' the roulette wheel. I was tellin' Mark about it, and he said he knew a way in here so we could take a look at the wheel." I shook my head. "I didn't have any earthly idea that a real detective was already on the trail."

"Well . . . no harm done, I suppose," Vince said with a smile.

"We'll run along now," I told him. "Come on, Mark."

For a second when I tugged on Mark's arm, I thought he was going to be stubborn and not come with me. I could tell he didn't like Vince's attitude, and I didn't blame him very much for that. But Vince worked for the attorney general, and I figured it would be better if he didn't know that Mark was a private eye investigating a case that was still open. I didn't know exactly what the law was concerning such things, but I had a pretty strong hunch the authorities frowned on it.

"Sure," Mark finally said with a grudging note in his voice. "Sorry if we got in the way of your investigation, Mallory."

"You didn't, not really," Vince said. He nodded toward the door behind the bar. "Go out the way you came in. I'd just as soon not alert the local cops that anything is going on in here. I don't want to get mixed up in any petty jurisdictional squabbles."

I couldn't claim to know Detective Travis all that well, but I had a feeling she might be pretty territorial when it came to the cases assigned to her. She wouldn't like it when she found out that the state was moving in and taking over, and I didn't blame Vince for wanting to postpone that showdown for as long as possible.

We left the casino, and as we walked along the narrow corridor between there and the kitchen, Mark said quietly but emphatically, "I'd like to give that smug kid a piece of my mind. He may be some hotshot investigator for the AG's office, but I was a detective when he was still in grade school."

"That's right," I said, "and you're not here to break up any crooked gambling ring or even to solve Ben Webster's murder. You're here to find out who's responsible for Hannah Kramer's death. That's what we'll concentrate on, from here on out."

"You still want to help me?" he asked as he glanced over at me in surprise.

"Sure. I like you, I like Louise, and heck, I guess

even Eddie's not all that bad. Hannah deserves justice, and so do her folks."

"I thought you were convinced the two murders are connected."

"Maybe they are," I said. "If that turns out to be the case, I reckon it'll all come out once the State Police start swarmin' over the boat, like Vince said. I'd rather see you solve the case, but the most important thing is findin' out the truth, right?"

"Right," Mark said, nodding. "I think we need to sit down with Louise and find out everything we can about Hannah. There's something out there that holds the key to her murder, if we can just figure out what it is." A grim look came over his face as he added, "I guess we'd better get Eddie in on this, too. It doesn't seem likely, but he might know something about Hannah that Louise doesn't."

I knew he was right, but the thought of sitting down with Eddie Kramer and discussing his daughter's murder didn't appeal to me. I knew by the look on Mark's face that he didn't care much for the idea, either.

But if we were going to find out the truth, we couldn't afford to overlook any possibilities— even one as big and obnoxious as Eddie Kramer.

CHAPTER 20

The dining room was full when we came out of the kitchen. It was lunchtime, I realized. With everything that had been going on, the morning had gotten away from me. The sight of all those people eating made my stomach growl quietly, reminding me that it had been a long time since that early breakfast.

"Why don't we get something to eat?" I suggested to Mark.

"I was about to say the same thing. Louise and Eddie are over there."

He had spotted the Kramers before I did, but now I saw them sitting at one of the tables. There were a couple of empty chairs, so I thought maybe they wouldn't mind if we joined them. We wouldn't bring up Hannah just yet, though. Talking about their daughter's murder wouldn't make for very good lunch conversation.

Louise looked up and smiled as we approached the table. "Eddie, look who's here," she said.

Eddie grunted. He didn't seem too happy to see us.

"Hello, there," I said as brightly as I could. "Would y'all mind if Mark and I joined you for lunch? It's sort of crowded in here."

There were other empty seats, but they couldn't very well turn us down if they wanted to be gracious. I figured that wasn't really a consideration for Eddie, but Louise answered without hesitation, "Of course. That will be nice, won't it, Eddie?"

"Sure," he said without any enthusiasm.

A waiter brought water as Mark and I sat down. Lunch was set up as a buffet, but he took our orders for iced tea to go with it. From the looks of the food on the plates in front of Eddie and Louise, they had just started eating and hadn't been here for long.

"You go ahead and get your food," I told Mark. "I'll wait until you get back."

He seemed to understand that I didn't want to give the Kramers a chance to slip away. He nodded and went to the buffet tables.

"Have you heard anything more about when we'll be able to leave?" Eddie asked.

I shook my head. "No. I know that Charles Gallister is on board and threatened Detective Travis with his lawyers, but that's the last I heard."

"It can't be too soon to suit me. Somebody's gonna be hearing from *my* lawyer when we get back home, I can tell you that much." He directed a meaningful glare at me.

Louise gave a nervous laugh and patted his

shoulder. "Oh, now, Eddie, don't go getting carried away. So it takes us a little longer to get
home than we thought it would. That's all right,
isn't it?"

He looked down at his plate. "Man's got
things he needs to do," he muttered.

"Of course you do," I said, "and I'm sorry for
any inconvenience that this delay causes, Mr.
Kramer. But sometimes things happen, and we
just have to accept them."

His head came up. He frowned. "What do
you mean by that?"

The sharpness of his tone made me realize
that I had pushed a little too hard, too soon. "Oh,
nothing," I said quickly. "That's just one of those
things people say sometimes."

Another grunt came from him. He went back
to eating, his jaw moving slowly and purpose-
fully as he chewed.

Mark came back to the table carrying a couple of plates, one with a salad on it, the other
piled high with spaghetti and sauce. Authentic
riverboat cuisine, I thought. I excused myself
and went to fill my own plates. That continued
the façade that we were just interested in lunch,
and besides I was really hungry.

When I got back to the table, I was surprised
to find that they were discussing Ben Webster's
murder. Only in general terms, though. I could
tell that Mark hadn't shared any of the information I had given him, such as the fact that Webster was really someone else.

"Whoever killed the guy must have really
hated him, to break his neck like that," Eddie

was saying. "It's not easy to do. They taught us how when I was a Marine." A harsh laugh came from him. "Hey, don't take that the wrong way. I'm not sayin' I broke Webster's neck. I didn't even know the kid."

"Oh, Eddie," Louise said, sounding nervous as usual when she was around him, like she was used to the fact that he might say or do just about anything. "You shouldn't go on so much."

He spread his hands. Big, powerful hands, I noted. "Hey, I'm just sayin'. When you kill somebody with your bare hands, you've got to have a mighty good reason to do it, that's all."

"There are only a few basic reasons for murder," Mark said. "Lust, greed, revenge . . ."

"Self-preservation," Eddie said.

"But that's self-defense, not murder," Mark replied.

Eddie shrugged. "Killin' is killin', when you get right down to it."

"I don't know that I'd agree with that," Mark said.

"Let's change the subject," Louise suggested.

Eddie wasn't ready to do that, though. He pointed across the table with his fork and went on, "People like to say that they don't know if they could ever take somebody else's life, but that's bull. Just about anybody will kill, if they've got a good enough reason. If somebody threatens you or your family . . . if somebody *hurts* your family . . . then they've got it comin' to 'em, I say."

"I can't disagree with that," Mark responded.

"And if they've got payback comin'," Eddie went on as his face reddened with anger, "if they hurt somebody you really love, then anybody with an ounce of humanity will try to settle the score with the lousy, no-good son of a—"

"Eddie, that's enough!" Louise said with an unaccustomed ferocity, and I couldn't help but recall how she had told me earlier that morning that she had come on the *Southern Belle* to kill somebody. She took a deep breath, calmed herself with a visible effort, and went on, "It doesn't do any good to get yourself all worked up like that."

"Nothin' does any good," Eddie said. He shoved his chair back and stood up. "Nothin' ever does any good." He turned and stalked toward the exit.

Louise gave us a helpless look and appealed to her old friend. "Mark . . ."

"It's time to come clean with him, Louise," he said. "You need to let him know who I really am. It might help."

"But . . . but I'm afraid of what he might have . . ."

She couldn't finish, but I had a pretty good idea what she meant. She was starting to be afraid that Eddie had taken the law into his own hands, that he had found out something linking Hannah with Ben Webster and had used that Marine training of his to break Webster's neck.

"Asking you to help me was a big mistake!" she blurted out as she looked across the table at Mark, confirming what I had just thought.

"It's too late now," Mark said as he stood up with a grim, determined look on his face. "I'm going to go talk to him."

Louise came to her feet, too, and caught hold of his arm. "You can't!"

"You don't want to make a scene, Louise," Mark said quietly.

She looked around her, saw that several people at nearby tables were watching with open curiosity, and with a sigh, she let go of Mark's arm.

I was standing by now, too, and I said, "Let's all go after Eddie and talk to him. I really think it'll be better to clear the air, Louise."

"I don't guess I have any choice," she murmured.

I glanced with regret at the food I was leaving behind. I hadn't gotten to eat much. But it was more important that we talk to Eddie Kramer, I told myself. The hard shell around him might be starting to crack, and who knew what we might find inside.

It might even be something we didn't want to find, like the fact that Eddie had killed Ben Webster.

When we came out on deck we looked both ways. "There he is," Louise said, pointing to the stairs leading up to the second deck. We went after him, but by the time we climbed to the second deck, Eddie was on his way to the third. We saw him turn toward the observation area on the bow when he reached the top of the stairs. That was where I had sat and talked with Vince Mallory earlier, when I'd had no idea that he was really a cop, too.

Eddie stood with his hands on the railing, peering out over the slow, majestic flow of the Mississippi. He was the only one up here at the moment. He didn't look around, but he seemed to know we were there as we came up behind him. He nodded toward the river and said, "Out there somewhere. That's where it happened."

Louise laid a hand on his arm and said, "Oh, Eddie . . ."

"In the dark," Eddie said, his voice choked with emotion. "That's maybe the worst of it. She couldn't see what was happening, she didn't know what was going on . . . God, she had to have been so scared."

Mark said, "She *didn't* know. She didn't feel anything after the first blow. It's not much, Eddie, but you can hang on to that much, anyway."

That made Eddie turn sharply from the railing, his hands clenching into fists. "What do *you* know about it?" he demanded. "You're just a damn actor!"

Mark stood easy, ready to defend himself if Eddie took a swing at him. He shook his head and said, "No, Eddie, I'm not an actor. I'm a private detective. Louise hired me to find out what really happened to Hannah."

Eddie's eyes widened. The struggle to accept what Mark was telling him was obvious to see on his face. After a moment he was able to say, "A detective?" He swung his gaze toward his wife. "You hired a detective?"

"You've heard me talk about Mark before," she said. I could tell she was struggling to stay calm, too. "Since the police hadn't found out anything, I thought maybe he could. He's working on the boat undercover."

Eddie's jaw clenched. A muscle jumped in it. "A detective," he said again. "I never would have guessed." He gave Mark a challenging look. "Well, what have you found out, shamus?"

"About Hannah's killer?" Mark shook his head. "I haven't figured out who it is yet. I'm not so sure about Ben Webster, though."

"Mark, no!" Louise said. "Eddie was just talking. He . . . he didn't mean anything."

Eddie let out a bark of laughter. "Is that what you're afraid of? That I killed that kid?"

Mark gave him a level stare. "You said it yourself, Eddie. If you found out that Ben Webster had something to do with Hannah's death, then he had it coming."

"Yeah, he would have . . . if that was what happened." Eddie made a slashing motion with his hand. "But as far as I know, the Webster kid didn't have anything to do with Hannah. He probably never even heard of her."

"He wasn't the guy she was dating in St. Louis?" Mark asked.

Eddie frowned at Mark. "Just how much do you know about my daughter, anyway?"

Louise said, "I told him everything, Eddie. Everything I could think of."

"That's why we came to talk to you," Mark said. "We figured it was time to clear the air and find out if you know anything Louise doesn't."

Eddie turned his head to look at me. "Let me

guess," he said with a half sneer. "You're a detective, too, Red."

Somebody calling me "Red" is one of my pet peeves. I admit that. Right then, however, I suppressed the irritation I felt and tried not to show Eddie how annoyed I was.

"No, I'm a travel agent," I told him. "I set up literary tours like this one. But I've got a stake in findin' out who killed Ben Webster. Havin' clients murdered while they're on one of my tours is bad for business."

"Yeah, I imagine so. How does that lady cop feel about you two sticking your noses into her case?"

"I don't reckon she'd like it," I said, "if she knew about it."

Eddie glanced back and forth between Mark and me with that defiant look on his face again. "So what is it you want from me?" he asked.

"We'd like to talk to you about Hannah," Mark said. His tone was quieter now, and not as confrontational. "Tell us everything you can about her life in St. Louis and her job here on the *Southern Belle.*"

"You said Louise already told you all about it."

"You might remember something she doesn't. And in a murder investigation, you never know what might turn out to be important . . . like the fact that Hannah was pregnant when she was killed," Mark said.

Louise paled, and Eddie's eyes narrowed dangerously. "Don't you even think about goin' around spreadin' dirt about my little girl," he said.

"I'm not spreading dirt," Mark said with a shake of his head. "We're the only ones up here. And the police already know about that, remember? It was in the autopsy report."

"Yeah, yeah," Eddie muttered. "That still doesn't mean I like people talking about it." He looked at Louise. "You told him?"

Her chin came up a little. "Of course I did. It might be important. And remember, Eddie, we lost a grandchild as well as a daughter. That's one more reason we need to find out who did that awful thing."

After a moment, he sighed and nodded. "You're right. Of course you're right. You always are."

Mark asked, "Do you have any idea who the baby's father was?"

"How would I know that if Louise didn't? Hannah talked to her a lot more than she ever talked to me." Eddie's heavy shoulders rose and fell in a shrug. "We never got along too good. Hannah had a mind of her own and didn't mind readin' somebody the riot act if she thought they were wrong, includin' her own dad." A tiny shadow of a wistful smile appeared on his face for a second, then was gone. "Louise always said we didn't get along because we were too much alike."

"The apple doesn't fall too far from the tree," Louise quoted softly.

"Yeah, whatever. Anyway, I can tell you what I *think*, even though I don't *know*. I think the baby's father was somebody at that fancy law firm."

"What law firm?" Mark asked with a frown.

"The one where Hannah worked for a couple of weeks as a temp before she got the job on this boat."

Mark looked at Louise. "You didn't say anything about her working at a law firm."

"I didn't think it was important," she said. "Like Eddie told you, it was just a temp job."

"Which firm was it?"

"Let me think. . . . There were three names, three partners, I suppose . . . ," Louise said.

Eddie said, "One of 'em was Pine, like the tree. I remember that."

"Winston, Pine, and Blevins," Mark said, his voice harsh with surprise.

"Yeah, that's it," Eddie said. "You've heard of the firm?"

Mark had done a lot more than hear of it, I thought. He had done a lot of work for Winston, Pine, and Blevins.

And not much more than an hour ago, someone from that firm had done his best to convince him to drop this case.

CHAPTER 21

Mark looked just as shocked as I felt. "You're sure about that?" he said. "Hannah worked for Winston, Pine, and Blevins?"

"Yeah," Eddie said. "And it wouldn't surprise me if it was one of those damn lawyers who got her pregnant. I never have liked lawyers, even my own."

Mark shook his head. "It wouldn't have been one of the partners," he said without a bit of doubt in his voice. "Leonard Winston is at least eighty years old and comes into the office only once or twice a year. Gerald Pine is the managing partner, but he's gay."

"What about Blevins?" I asked.

"John Blevins is dead. His wife still shares in the firm's profits, but no one from his family practices there. None of his kids are even lawyers."

"What about associates?" Eddie asked. "Don't most big law firms like that have a lot of associates working for them?"

Mark nodded. "Yes, there are about a dozen associates. I don't even know all of them."

"And *you* seem to know a lot about the place," Eddie said as he frowned in a vaguely accusing manner at Mark.

"Eddie!" Louise said. "You can't be serious. I've known Mark since I was a girl. I hired him to help us, for gosh sake."

Eddie didn't pay any attention to her. He continued glaring at Mark and demanded, "How about it? What's your connection with those lawyers?"

"I do investigative work for them." Mark amended, "Or rather, I *did* investigative work for them. I think I got fired a little while ago."

"Why?"

"Because I refused to stop working on your daughter's case and run back to St. Louis to take on a job for them."

Eddie snorted. "Don't make it sound so blasted noble. You couldn't have gone anyway, as long as the cops have us stuck here."

That comment made a couple of things click together in my head. I put a hand on Mark's arm and said, "They called you out of the blue with that other case?"

He turned to look at me. "Yeah, Mr. Pine said the client asked for me."

"Has that ever happened before?"

Mark thought about it for a second, then said, "No, not that I recall. Most clients wouldn't know who I was. They just come to the firm for results and don't really care how they go about getting them."

"So it would have to be a regular client, somebody who knew who you were. Somebody who might recognize you if they saw you."

"Well, once you think about it like that, what you're saying makes sense," Mark admitted.

"Let me make a wild guess," I said. "The biggest client the firm has is Charles Gallister."

Mark's mouth tightened into a hard line. "Yeah, that's probably right," he said.

"Would Gallister know you by sight?"

"Maybe. I've been introduced to him once or twice, but it's been a while."

"And this fella Pine would want to give Gallister whatever he asked for, right?"

"Oh, yeah," Mark said. "There are a lot of billable hours at stake in giving Charles Gallister whatever he wants."

I lifted a finger and poked at the air as I put my thoughts into words. "So Gallister sees you when he comes on board the *Southern Belle* earlier today and recognizes you as a private detective. He was already going to call his lawyers—Winston, Pine, and Blevins—and raise holy Ned about the riverboat being stuck here in Hannibal, and oh, by the way, while he's talking to them he also tells them he needs you, you in particular, to work on some unspecified case for him. He's anticipating that they're gonna be able to get a court order releasing the boat and the passengers, so you can hotfoot it back to St. Louis and forget all about the case that brought you up here. Does that make sense?"

"It does," Mark said as he nodded. "Some of it

is pure speculation, but it hangs together all right."

Eddie and Louise had been listening and frowning as they tried to follow what I was saying, and now Eddie spoke up. "Yeah, but what does it *mean?*"

"When Gallister saw Mark and remembered that he's a private eye, he probably figured that he was here workin' on a case," I said. "Ben Webster's murder happened after the cruise started. There's only one unsolved case involving the *Southern Belle* that could have brought Mark up here."

"Hannah's murder," Louise breathed.

I nodded. "Gallister decided you must be working on Hannah's case," I said to Mark, "and he didn't want you here. So he tried to get his lawyers to call you off and decoy you away on something else."

"Why would he do that?" Louise asked.

Mark didn't have time to answer before Eddie said, "That son of a bitch." His voice rose in a roar. "*That son of a bitch!*"

He stomped toward the stairs.

Mark caught hold of his arm and stopped him. Eddie turned fast, swinging a punch at Mark with his other arm. That Marine training of Eddie's was probably pretty good, but it had been a long time ago. He had spent the years since then as a businessman while Mark had been working as a private eye, which was probably a lot more strenuous. And Mark was just in better shape to start with. He blocked the punch, swung Eddie around, and twisted his arm behind his back.

"Take it easy," Mark said. "I don't want to hurt you, Eddie."

"Let me go," Eddie panted. "Lemme go, dammit! I'll kill the son of a bitch!"

Louise got in front of him and put her hands on his shoulders. "Calm down, Eddie," she said. "You've got to calm down. It's not going to do any good for you to go flying off the handle like you always do."

Her words seemed to get through to him. He took a couple of deep, ragged breaths, then jerked his head in a nod. "All right, Lansing, you can let go of me," he said. "I won't do anything."

"You'd better not be lying to me," Mark said as he released Eddie's arm. Eddie brought it back around in front of him and rubbed it where the muscles must have been pulled.

Louise turned to Mark. "Do you really think Charles Gallister could have had something to do with Hannah's death? A rich man like that?"

"Rich men break the law, too, all the time," he said. He looked at me. "But Delilah's the one who came up with this theory. Let's give her a chance to talk it out."

"Thanks," I said. "What do you know about Gallister? Is he the sort of man who'd take up with a young woman like Hannah?"

Mark grunted. "Gallister's the sort of man who'd take up with anybody if she was female and reasonably attractive."

"Hannah was a beautiful young woman," Louise said quietly.

"She certainly was," Mark agreed. "From the gossip I heard about Gallister around the firm, all the secretaries knew not to let themselves get caught alone in an elevator with him. The female associates were the same way, although I think some of them probably played up to him to try to advance their careers. He has a reputation as a lecher, though."

"So a pretty girl from a small town, living on her own in the city for the first time, working as a temp . . . she'd be a prime target for a man like Gallister?" I asked.

"Oh, yeah," Mark said. "I never knew that there was a connection between Hannah and the law firm, or I might have thought of Gallister. He was there in the offices a lot, consulting with Gerald Pine. He could have seen Hannah and set his sights on her—"

Eddie growled. Literally growled. Louise put a hand on his arm to calm him.

"He wouldn't have been able to resist the challenge," Mark went on. "He's the sort of man who thinks he can charm any woman he wants to."

I recalled him trying that charm on Detective Travis. When it hadn't worked, Gallister had gotten angry. Hannah's condition when she was murdered, though, seemed to indicate that Gallister's efforts had been successful where she was concerned—*if* there was anything to this except blue sky.

"Let's say he meets her at the law firm, he goes after her, and she falls for his line," I said. "He gets her the job on this boat. Easy enough for him to do, since he owns the *Southern Belle*. Then she turns up pregnant. What would she do then?"

"If you're thinking that she would try to blackmail him, you're wrong," Louise said. "Hannah would never do such a thing."

As gently as he could, Mark said, "You can't be sure about that, Louise—"

"But I am," she insisted. "I knew my daughter, Mark. She wasn't a blackmailer."

"And you're probably right about that," I told her. "But Gallister didn't know her that well. If he found out she was pregnant, he could have been afraid that she'd try to shake him down, whether she actually would have or not."

Eddie said, "Does this guy Gallister already have a wife?"

Mark nodded. "He does. She comes from old money, too. That's how Gallister got his start in business. He charmed the right woman."

"Does she know he plays around?"

"I'm not privy to their private life," Mark said, "but again, going by gossip, she knows. That's why she hasn't been completely sober for a lot of years now. But they're still married, and I'll bet Gallister would take quite a financial hit if they weren't together anymore."

Eddie started toward the stairs. "Where's that lady cop? We've got to tell her all this before Gallister has a chance to get away."

"Wait a minute," I told him. "We can't prove any of it. We're just talking about what might have happened."

Eddie glared at Mark. "You're a detective. *Get* proof."

"A year after the crime, I'm not sure how we're going to do that," Mark said. "Anyway, if Gallister wanted to get rid of Hannah, he wouldn't do it himself. He'd hire it done, and he'd use a professional. If we're right about this, whoever actually killed her is probably long gone. They could be halfway around the world by now."

"I don't care about that. Gallister would be the one who's really responsible for what happened. He's got to pay," Eddie replied.

"If he's guilty," Mark said. He frowned in thought for a moment and then grimaced. "There's one thing I can think of that we can do. . . ."

"Then we should do it," Louise said.

"It's not pleasant," Mark warned.

Eddie snapped, "Nothing about your daughter being murdered is pleasant. What's your idea, Lansing?"

"You could have Hannah's body exhumed and have DNA testing done on the baby she was carrying. Then, if you could get a DNA sample from Gallister, you could see if there was a match. You couldn't actually prove he was the father that way—DNA's not as exact as most people like to think it is—but you *could* determine whether the father was either Gallister or a close male relative of his. And since, as far as I know, he doesn't have any male relatives that close"—

Mark shrugged—"that would be enough proof for a jury, if it turned out the DNA matched. There's only one problem."

"What's that?" Louise asked.

"Getting Gallister to give you a DNA sample. If he knows that he was the father of Hannah's baby, he's going to guess right away why you want it, and he'll balk."

"Make him cooperate," Eddie said. "Get a court order."

Mark shook his head. "He's got one of the biggest and best law firms in the Midwest working for him. Actually, it's one of the best in the whole country. If you file a civil action against him and try to force him to give you a DNA sample that way, he'll fight it as long as his money holds out . . . and that's going to be a lot longer than yours does."

I saw Eddie's shoulders slump and said, "Wouldn't that be the same as him admitting it, if he wouldn't cooperate?"

"Not legally. You can't force a man to give you his DNA if he doesn't want to, not without a judge on your side."

"What about the cops?" I asked. "If they went after him—"

"First you'd have to convince them to investigate him," Mark said, "and based on the evidence we have, which is pretty much nothing, I don't think you'd have any luck with that. Even if you did manage to interest the police, Gallister would fight just as hard to prevent the DNA test, and he'd drag it out for years, maybe."

"What if you—"

He held up a hand to stop me. "Got a DNA sample without him being aware of it? Dug through his trash and found a cup or a napkin or something with his saliva on it?"

Louise made a face. So did I. It was a pretty distasteful idea.

"It wouldn't be admissible as evidence," Mark went on. "Too much opportunity for the sample to be tainted or manipulated somehow. That's why the cops place so much importance on the chain of evidence."

"Well, then, what the hell *can* we do?" Eddie burst out.

Mark smiled. "We have to spook Gallister into making a mistake."

"How do we do that?" Louise asked.

"You say that Hannah wouldn't have blackmailed him," Mark told her, "and you're probably right about that. But that doesn't mean *I* can't blackmail him."

CHAPTER 22

"Dadgum it!" I said. "You're talkin' about puttin' a target smack-dab on your back and hopin' that he takes a shot at it!"

Mark shrugged. "If you've got a better idea, I'm willing to listen."

That was just the problem. I *didn't* have a better idea. Everything else I had come up with, he had already shot down.

"I don't get it," Eddie said.

"Mark's going to tell Mr. Gallister he knows who the father of Hannah's baby was," Louise said. She had picked up right away on the plan, too. "He'll imply that Mr. Gallister had . . . had Hannah killed to keep her from telling anyone that she was pregnant by him."

She had trouble getting the words out, and I didn't blame her. She'd had to accept a lot of terrible things over the past year. It looked like the end might finally be in sight, though. With luck, Louise might get the closure she needed.

But if we were right about Hannah and Gallister, I didn't see any connection between that case and Ben Webster's murder. My instincts kept coming back there and trying to forge some sort of link between them. For the life of me, though, I couldn't see what it might be.

Eddie faced Mark and said, "If you do that, Gallister's liable to have *you* killed."

"He can try," Mark said with a shrug. "Doesn't mean he'll succeed. If he makes a move against me, that might be enough to convince the cops we're right about him. Convicting him of Hannah's murder will still be a long, hard fight, but at least it'll be a start."

"You'd do that?" Eddie asked. "You'd put yourself in danger to help get justice for my little girl?"

"That's the job I was hired to do."

Louise touched his arm. "You know that not everybody would go to such lengths for their job, Mark. You're doing this for Eddie and me, not just for Hannah."

"Well . . ." Mark shrugged.

Eddie stuck out a hand. "I'm sorry I took a swing at you, pal. I was outta my head because I was so mad at that jerk Gallister. Truce?"

"Sure," Mark said as he gripped Eddie's hand.

The sound of footsteps on the stairs leading up to the third deck made me turn and look. I saw a black cap rising along them, then the lean, weathered face of Captain L. B. Williams came into view.

"I've been looking for you, Mr. Lansing," the

captain said as he came out onto the observation deck.

Uh-oh, I thought. Gallister must have told Williams that Mark had gotten the job as Mark Twain under false pretenses. The captain was probably here to fire him.

Instead, to my surprise, Williams went on, "Since it appears that we're going to be delayed here in Hannibal until tomorrow, I'd like for you to do another performance as Mark Twain tonight in the salon."

"Wait just a minute," Eddie said, and I didn't know if the upset look on his face was an act or if that was just his natural personality asserting itself again. "What do you mean we're still stuck here?"

Williams looked like he had just bitten into something sour. "Mr. Gallister's attorneys have had more difficulty than they anticipated in obtaining a court order releasing the *Southern Belle* from the custody of the Hannibal police. It seems that the judge they planned to approach with their request is ill at the moment."

I found it hard to believe that a firm the size of Winston, Pine, and Blevins had only one judge in their back pocket, but since this was actually a stroke of luck for us, I wasn't going to complain about it. With another night in Hannibal, we'd have more time to try to prod Charles Gallister into making a mistake—assuming that he was still on board. A glance at the parking area told me that the car he'd arrived in was still there, indicating that he hadn't left the riverboat.

I tried to confirm that by saying to Williams, "I'm surprised that Gallister hasn't gone back down to St. Louis himself to raise heck."

"I wouldn't presume to speak for Mr. Gallister," Williams replied stiffly. "I assume he feels that he can do more good here, trying to persuade the local authorities that they should release the boat."

So he was definitely still on board. That was good.

"I'll be glad to do the performance, Captain," Mark said. "The usual time?"

"That will be fine." Williams gave us all a curt nod, then turned and went to the stairs. We watched in silence as he climbed to the pilot-house.

Once we were alone again on the observation deck, Louise said, "I thought for sure he was going to tell you that he knows you're a private detective, Mark."

"Yeah," Eddie agreed. "I figured Gallister told him."

"We don't *know* that Gallister recognized me," Mark reminded them—and me, since the same thought had crossed my mind. "Right now it's just a theory. One that the facts seem to support, though."

"Yeah, and if he did recognize you, then he's keeping it to himself," I said as I mulled over what had just happened. "Actually, this supports what we were thinking, because if he's guilty of something, he wouldn't want anybody else knowing that there's a private eye on board. If they did, they might ask Gallister why that would be."

Mark thought about it and then nodded. "Yeah, that makes sense. It's in his best interest to keep everything relating to Hannah's murder as quiet as possible."

"And since he saw you without your Mark Twain getup on, he probably doesn't know you're the one who does the performances in the salon," I went on. "Williams came looking for you and asked you to do that tonight on his own, not because Gallister told him to."

Mark looked closely at me for a couple of seconds, then said, "I may not know you all that well yet, Delilah, but I've got a hunch you're up to something. You've got some sort of plan in mind, don't you?"

"Maybe," I said. "How does this sound?"

Considering how packed with activity the past twenty-four hours had been, the rest of that afternoon was strangely uneventful. With the casino and the salon closed and all the passengers confined to the boat, most folks holed up in their cabins and read or slept or sat around and complained, for all I knew. A few of them strolled the decks, obviously determined to get some fresh air and exercise even if they couldn't go sightseeing in Hannibal, which sat there in plain sight but for the moment out of reach of everybody on the *Southern Belle*.

Mark and I told Louise and Eddie to leave

everything to us. They went back to their cabin, and we went to Mark's. We had just come in the door when my phone rang. It was Melissa again, asking me about that information she had for me on my stolen computer. I made writing motions at Mark, and he handed me a pen and a piece of paper. I jotted down the numbers Melissa gave me, then told her, "See what you can find out about Charles Gallister."

"Who?"

"The owner of this boat. He's some sort of Midwest real estate mogul, too."

"Why do you need to know that?" Melissa asked. Before I could answer, she went on, "Never mind. I'll bet you're trying to do some detective work again, aren't you?"

"You're the one who keeps tellin' me stuff that makes me curious," I told her.

"Be careful, Mom. Remember what almost happened to you on that plantation."

"I'm not likely to forget it," I said. Nearly getting stabbed tends to stick in your mind. "Call me back with whatever you find, okay?"

"Sure. You want the dirt, right?"

"The dirtier, the better," I told her.

That statement made Mark raise his eyebrows quizzically.

"I was talking about Gallister," I explained as I closed the phone. "Melissa's gonna try to find out if he's had any legal problems in the past."

"If he has, I'm sure they've been well covered up by Gerald Pine."

"Yeah, but the Internet's a wonderful thing. You never know what you're gonna find."

We sat down with Mark's books by and about Mark Twain and began looking for things he could use in his performance that night. Getting Gallister to attend might be tricky, but it was important that he be there. Mark's performance was going to set him up for the blackmail later.

"You know," I said as a new worry occurred to me, "you might get arrested and accused of being a real blackmailer. The cops might not believe you if you told them you were just tryin' to spook Gallister into revealin' his involvement with Hannah's murder."

"That's a chance I'll have to take," he said. "How about this one? 'Laws are sand, customs are rock. Laws can be evaded and punishment escaped, but an openly transgressed custom brings sure punishment.' "

"That might work," I said as I paged through one of the volumes. "Here's another one: 'One of the most striking differences between a cat and a lie is that a cat has only nine lives.' Gallister's a liar. I reckon we can be pretty sure of that."

"Being a liar and being a murderer are two different things."

"Mark Twain said that?"

"No," Mark said. "I did. Huck Finn said, 'All kings is mostly rapscallions.' Gallister is a king of sorts, at least in his own mind. He's used to doing what he wants and getting away with it."

"Yeah, well, that's about to come to an end," I predicted with more confidence than I felt.

* * *

Late that afternoon I left Mark working on his monologue for that night's performance and went up to the pilothouse. I ignored the AU-THORIZED PERSONNEL ONLY sign on the stairs—I was getting good at that—and marched right up there. When I opened the door and stepped inside, I was struck by how nice the place was. Just a short time earlier in Mark's cabin, I had read a description of a pilothouse in *Life on the Mississippi*:

". . . showy red and gold window curtains; an imposing sofa; leather cushions and a back to the high bench where visiting pilots sit, to spin yarns and 'look at the river'; bright, fanciful 'cuspidores,' instead of a broad wooden box filled with sawdust; nice new oilcloth on the floor; a hospitable big stove for winter; a wheel as high as my head, costly with inlaid work; a wire tiller-rope; bright brass knobs for the bells."

I won't try to fool you into thinking that I recalled all that from memory; I went and looked it up. But it was in my mind at that moment as I looked around the interior of the *Southern Belle*'s pilothouse. Not everything in there was the same as in Twain's description, of course. There were no cuspidors, nor a wood-burning stove. The floor was highly polished wood instead of being covered with oilcloth. But there were big windows with bright curtains pulled back at the moment, to give a sweeping view all around of the river and the town of Hannibal, and a high, red leather chair where the captain sat, and most of all the wheel, tall and wide and impressive with its brass fittings and its smooth, burnished wood and the sense of power that went with it because all you had to do was look at it to know that it controlled not only the course of this boat but also its destiny.

Of course, at the moment it had nothing to do because the boat was docked and wasn't going anywhere until a judge or Detective Travis gave the word, and I didn't expect either of those things to happen until the next day, at the earliest.

Captain Williams swung around in the tall swivel chair. He was the only person in the pilothouse and looked surprised to see me.

"Ms. Dickinson," he said. "You're not supposed to be up here. What can I do for you?"

I smiled. "I sort of wanted to see what things look like from up here. You've got the best view on the boat, don't you?"

"The pilot does. The boat is in his hands. The captain merely gives the orders."

"Oh, I'll bet you do more than that." I sensed that he wasn't going to respond to any flirting, so I made my tone more businesslike as I went on, "I was hopin', too, that you could tell me where to find Mr. Gallister. He *is* still on the boat, isn't he?"

"He is," Williams replied with a frown. "I'm not sure it would be a good idea to disturb him, though. He's been on the phone with his attorneys all afternoon, and he's rather upset about their lack of progress."

"Well, then, he needs a break," I said. "Mark Lansing is working up a special show for tonight, so I thought I'd invite Mr. Gallister."

"I'm not sure he'd be interested—" Williams began.

"Oh, it'll do him good," I insisted. "I don't think he'll turn me down if I ask him personally."

"Hmmmph," the captain said. I had a pretty good idea what he was thinking. He was bound to know about Gallister's reputation as a womanizer, and clearly he didn't approve of it. But after a moment he went on, "Mr. Gallister is in his private suite. He keeps it for use here on the boat. He's quite interested in the riverboat era, you know. Much of the décor on the *Southern Belle* was suggested by him."

So that was why some of it looked like it came out of a fancy whorehouse, I thought, but I kept that notion to myself. I also couldn't help but wonder what Gallister had used his private suite for in the past. I figured I had a pretty good idea.

"If you could just tell me where to find that suite . . ."

He hesitated, and I could tell that he didn't really want to answer my question. But then he said, "It's on the third deck. Go past the offices and you'll find an unmarked door. That leads into an anteroom. But I must insist on one thing, Ms. Dickinson, if you want to bring any more tours on the *Southern Belle* . . ."

"What's that, Captain?"

"I didn't tell you where to find him," he said

in a flat, hard voice. I knew in that moment that Captain Williams didn't like Charles Gallister. Gallister might own the *Southern Belle*, but in the captain's mind, the riverboat belonged to *him.* He probably didn't like seeing it used as a gambling den, and he dang sure didn't like Gallister bringing his girlfriends on it.

"He won't hear it from me, Captain. I give you my word."

Williams nodded. "Good luck to you, then." He paused. "You may need it."

For some reason I felt like a nice, juicy little lamb about to enter the lion's den.

CHAPTER 23

I didn't have any trouble finding the door Captain Williams had described to me. No one tried to stop me, either. The crew seemed to have gotten more lax in carrying out their duties since we'd been stuck here. I think everybody was upset about it.

I felt sorry for the captain, too. He paled into insignificance when Charles Gallister came aboard. Not only that, but even though he didn't know it yet, things were about to get even worse for him once the state attorney general launched that crooked gambling probe Vince Mallory had mentioned to Mark and me in the casino. I didn't think for a second that Williams had anything to do with the criminal operation or even knew about it, but that wouldn't prevent him from being disgraced along with all the other people involved in running the boat.

Mark and I ought to just back off and let Vince and the other investigators from the AG's office go about their business, I told myself.

They would solve Ben Webster's murder, and once they started bringing out the rest of the dirty laundry involving the *Southern Belle*, there was a good chance they would solve Hannah's murder, too, and nail Charles Gallister for it even though he might not be any more involved with the crooked gambling than Captain Williams was.

But somehow that just didn't feel right. Hannah's death was a very personal killing. Bad enough that someone had hit her like that. Then they had laid their hands on her, carried her to the railing, and pitched her off into the river where the paddlewheel would mangle her body. It took a special sort of monster to do something like that—and a monster to arrange it, too, because I still believed that Gallister wouldn't have dirtied his own hands by carrying out the murder. The people who had been hurt the most, other than Hannah herself, of course, ought to be the ones who brought him to justice, not some investigators paid by the state who had never even known Hannah.

Of course, *I* hadn't known Hannah, I reminded myself, but I knew Louise and Eddie. Mark and I were acting on their behalf in trying to trap Gallister. We weren't working for the state, or even for society at large.

Murder was personal. Justice should be, too.

With that thought in mind, I opened the door, stepped into the anteroom, and knocked on the door of Charles Gallister's private suite.

There was no response, so after a minute I knocked again, harder this time. A few more seconds went by, and then Gallister himself jerked the door open and demanded, "What is it?"

He had taken off the jacket of the ridiculously expensive suit but still wore the vest. He'd loosened his tie as well, and in his left hand he held a short, squat glass made of thick crystal with a couple of inches of amber liquid in it. Gallister's flushed face told me that drink wasn't the first one he'd had recently.

As soon as he saw me, the irritation vanished from his features and was replaced by a smile. "Well, well," he went on. "Exactly what I like to see when I open my door: a beautiful woman."

I had a feeling that he would have said the same thing to just about any female between the ages of eighteen and sixty. Maybe a year or two either side of that. I smiled back at him as if I enjoyed hearing it, even though, smug, would-be Lotharios like Gallister annoyed the heck out of me, like they did for most women.

"Have we met, my dear?" he asked.

That was a good way to endear yourself to somebody, I thought—openly acknowledge that you couldn't even remember if you'd met the person before. But I just said, "Not exactly. My name is Delilah Dickinson."

"A lovely, lovely name." He made a sweeping motion with the glass in his hand. "Won't you come in?"

I stepped into the suite's sitting room, getting that old lion's den feeling again as I did so. As Gallister firmly closed the door behind me, he continued, "What can I do for you, Delilah?"

He didn't even ask if he could call me by my

given name, I noticed. Again, I didn't allow my expression or my voice to reveal that that bothered me. Instead I said, "I run Dickinson Literary Tours. I have a group here on the boat."

"Of course. I remember seeing you on deck earlier. I was going to ask Captain Williams to tell me your name, but then I got distracted with this terrible business about the murder and all. Still, I shouldn't allow anything to distract me from finding out more about a beautiful woman."

He had a twinkle in his eye as he said it. Obviously, he planned to keep hitting that "beautiful woman" note. I didn't know if he was doing it because he actually found me attractive, or because it was just habit with him. I wasn't sure I wanted to know.

"What brings you here to my suite?" he asked. I was glad he didn't want to know how I'd found out where it was. That way I didn't have to lie *or* get Captain Williams into trouble.

"I just wanted to thank you for your efforts to get the police to release the riverboat. A lot of my clients would like to get back home or get on with the rest of their vacations."

Gallister grimaced and shrugged. "I appreciate the sentiment, my dear, but I haven't done much good in that respect so far. That police detective is one stubborn . . . I mean, Detective Travis is being adamant that she doesn't want the *Southern Belle* to leave Hannibal until she's had a chance to investigate the murder more fully. My attorneys have run into some unexpected roadblocks in circumventing that order. But I'm confident that they'll be successful before too much longer. Can I offer you a drink?"

"No, thanks," I said.

"Come on," he urged with a grin. "The sun's over the yardarm. And I have some excellent Kentucky bourbon."

I didn't tell him that the same thought about the yardarm had crossed my mind earlier in the day. I said, "No, I really can't. I had another reason for stoppin' by, though."

He sipped his whiskey, then asked, "And what might that be?"

"I want to invite you to come down to the salon at eight tonight for a special performance." I remembered that Gallister was supposed to be a Mark Twain buff, although I was convinced that his main reason for owning this riverboat was so he'd have someplace he could shack up with his girlfriends from time to time. "Mr. Mark Twain himself will be there."

Gallister grinned. "Old Sam Clemens, eh? You're a fan of Twain's work?"

"Of course I am. Would I be leading a tour group on this cruise otherwise?"

Actually, whether I was a fan of a particular writer didn't matter one way or the other. A tour might be profitable regardless of my opinion of the author's work. I was more interested in the bottom line, although I do have a liking for most Southern literature.

"So you'll be there?" Gallister asked.

"With bells on," I said.

"I like that image," he said. As he smiled at me, I had the uncomfortable feeling that he was picturing me with bells on—and not much else.

I hurried on, "So you'll be there?"

"Definitely," he said. "Assuming that that bulldog of a policewoman will allow us into the salon by then."

I hadn't thought about that. Detective Travis had closed the salon for the day, but surely by now she was getting close to being finished with the interviews she was conducting with the passengers and crew. If the salon remained off limits, Mark wouldn't be able to put on his performance after all.

Of course, he didn't have to in order for us to proceed with our plan. The special material he planned to include in the show was meant to soften up Gallister, that's all. We could go ahead without it.

"Don't worry, I'll speak to the detective again," Gallister went on. "Now that I know you'll be in attendance tonight, I won't allow anything to interfere with the show."

"That's mighty kind of you," I told him.

"It's the least I can do." He frowned in thought. "Let me see. . . . That young man who was killed, he was a member of your tour group, wasn't he?"

"That's right. Ben Webster." I paused. "You didn't happen to know him, did you?"

"Me?" Gallister looked and sounded genuinely surprised. "Why would I know him?"

"Oh, no reason. But surely, people you're acquainted with come on this boat from time to time."

"Certainly. I recommend it to all my friends and business acquaintances." He chuckled. "I've let some potential customers in real estate deals take the cruise for free. One of the perks of being the owner."

Like getting one of your girlfriends a job here— until she turned up pregnant, I thought.

"But I never heard of this young fellow Webster," Gallister went on. "I leave all the details of booking the cruises to people who are good at that. I've learned over the years to get good people to handle things and then get out of their way and let them do their jobs. Captain Williams tends to the running of the boat, Logan Rafferty supervises security and the casino, Ted Simmons is in charge of the kitchen . . . you get the idea."

I nodded and said, "Captain Williams looks like he would've been right at home in Mark Twain's day, steaming up and down the Mississippi."

"He certainly does. He's a throwback, in a way. So is Rafferty. He should have been in Las Vegas in the forties and fifties."

"Mobster, eh?"

Gallister put a finger on the tip of his nose, pushed it to one side, and grinned.

"Well, if you ever need anybody killed . . ." I said.

"I'll know who to go to!" Gallister finished with a laugh. Suddenly, he looked sober as he realized what we had just said. "Now, wait just a minute. I didn't mean for that to sound like . . . I mean, what with that murder that happened yesterday . . . I know that Logan had nothing to do with it. I'm certain of that."

"Oh, so am I," I said. "How long has he worked here on the *Southern Belle?*"

"Three years. Ever since I bought the boat and had it restored."

"So he was here when that murder happened last year."

I worried that I might be jumping the gun and pushing Gallister too hard, but he seemed talkative at the moment. He was still trying to impress me, I thought, and he might not be that way with a lot of other people around, like at the performance in the salon tonight—if the performance even took place.

Gallister looked at me blankly. "What murder?"

"I don't know all the details," I said. "I just heard somebody talkin' about it. Some girl who worked as a cocktail waitress in the casino. She was hit on the head and thrown overboard. . . ."

"Oh, yes, that dreadful business. I remember it vaguely. What was her name again?"

I didn't answer. If I had just heard rumors about the case, as I'd told him, then it was likely I wouldn't know Hannah's name.

"Helen?" he went on. "Hester? I remember it was some sort of old-fashioned name . . . Hannah! That's it. Hannah Kramer. I remember her now."

You ought to, I thought. *You were sleeping with her.*

"Nice girl. Very attractive, as I recall. It's a real shame about what happened to her."

"It would have been a shame even if she hadn't been very attractive," I said.

"Of course, of course. That's not what I meant. When Logan told me about it, I instructed him to cooperate fully with the police."

"But they never found out who killed her, did they?"

"No, not that I'm aware of." Gallister made a face again. "I hope the *Southern Belle* doesn't get a reputation as a bad-luck boat because of this new murder. If you and the other tour operators start thinking that she's jinxed, it'll ruin business."

"Well, you've always got real estate to fall back on," I said.

"That's right, I do." He tossed back the rest of his drink. "Is there anything else I can do for you, Delilah?"

"No, that's all," I said. "I'll see you in the salon at eight, assumin' that Detective Travis lets us in there again?"

"I'll be there," he promised. He held out a hand. I took it, and for a second I thought he was going to kiss the back of my hand. He settled for shaking it, though, and he didn't hold on for more than a few seconds longer than he had to. I saw a distracted look in his eyes, and I had to wonder if it was there because I had brought up Hannah's murder. He had to be worried that Webster's murder would draw attention to that year-old, unsolved case.

He put a hand lightly on my arm as we went

to the door of the suite. He opened it and ush-
ered me into the anteroom. "Good-bye until
later, Delilah," he said. "Remember, you're always welcome on the *Southern Belle.*"

"Thanks. I hope to be bringin' plenty of tours
on this cruise in the future."

He closed the door of his suite, and I opened
the door leading from the anteroom to the
deck. I stepped out and nearly ran smack-dab
into a mountain.

A mountain named Logan Rafferty.

CHAPTER 24

If I had run into him, I figure I would have bounced right off that broad chest of his. As it was, I came to a stop just inches from him, and I was immediately uncomfortable at having our personal spaces jammed together like that. I took a step back into the anteroom.

"Ms. Dickinson," Rafferty said. "How are you?"

"Fine, I reckon," I said. I didn't want to stand around making small talk with Rafferty. I wanted to get back to Mark's cabin.

"No offense, but what are you doing here?" he asked. "This area is off limits to passengers." Before I could answer, he went on, "Ah, yes, I remember. You don't consider yourself a regular passenger."

"I was just talking to Mr. Gallister," I said.

"About . . . ?"

I frowned. "Well, no offense to you, either, Mr. Rafferty, but I don't reckon that's any of your business."

"Everything that happens on this boat is my

business, Ms. Dickinson," he said, his voice little more than a silky, dangerous whisper. "As a matter of fact, I was looking for you."

"Me?" I said. "What for?"

"There's something I'd like to show you, down below decks where Ben Webster's body was found."

That surprised me. I figured that the police had already found everything there was to be found at the crime scene, and I assumed that as a crime scene, it was still off limits. But that storage locker was near the engine room, I recalled, and the engine room personnel used the equipment in it from time to time, so it made sense that the police would try to make it accessible to the crew again as soon as possible.

On the other hand, the *Southern Belle* wasn't actually *going* anywhere until the cops gave the okay, so the main engines weren't running, only the generators that provided power for the lights, air-conditioning, etc.

"If you found something that might be important to the case," I said to Rafferty, "you need to show it to Detective Travis, not to me."

Rafferty shook his head. "She's not on board right now. She finished questioning everybody and left a little while ago."

"But we're still not free to go?" Maybe Gallister's attorneys had been successful at last, and Gallister just didn't know about it.

"Not yet," Rafferty said with a disgusted look. "Anyway, we wouldn't start back to St. Louis tonight, even if the cops said it was okay."

I looked past him, which wasn't easy since he

filled up nearly all the doorway between the anteroom and the deck. The rosy light was fading
in the sky, which told me the sun had set. It was
later than I had thought.

"Whatever you found, I'm sure you could call
Detective Travis—" I began.

Rafferty stopped me with an emphatic shake
of his head. "No, not until I'm sure what I've got
is really important. That's why I want you to have
a look at it."

"Me? What do I have to do with it, whatever *it*
is?"

"Webster was a member of your tour group."

"Which doesn't mean a blasted thing. I never
met him before yesterday."

Rafferty leaned closer to me. I didn't like it,
but there wasn't really anyplace I could retreat.

"If I'm right about what I suspect," he said,
"then Webster wasn't really who he said he was."

That surprised me, too. I already knew that
"Ben Webster" had been a phony identity, but
how had Rafferty found out about that?

Maybe the same way Melissa had, I thought.
Maybe he had searched around enough on the
Internet to stumble over Webster's deception.

But it was the phony billing address on the
credit card that had tipped Melissa off in the
first place, and Rafferty wouldn't have had that
information, I reminded myself. Whatever Rafferty had uncovered, it was something new.

"All right," I said. "I'll take a look at it."

He smiled. "Good. Come with me."

Go below decks alone with a man whom
Charles Gallister had just likened to a Vegas

gangster, a man I strongly suspected might have had something to do with at least one murder and maybe two? I wasn't born yesterday. I smiled at Rafferty and said, "Fine, but let's get the captain to go down there with us."

Rafferty shook his head. "I don't want to bother the captain with this. Let's figure out first if it really means anything."

"Sorry," I told him. "I'm not goin' anywhere with you unless somebody comes with us." I started to turn back toward the door of the suite. "I'll see if Mr. Gallister would like to be part of this."

"You've talked to Gallister enough," Rafferty said.

The tone of his voice warned me, but I didn't have time to react. As he spoke, his hand came down hard on my left shoulder. I tried to twist away and opened my mouth to yell, but before any sound could emerge, his other hand clamped over the whole lower half of my face. He jerked me back against him, which was sort of like being jerked against a brick wall.

"You've stirred up enough trouble," he rasped into my ear as he put his head close to mine. "You and your damn partner are gonna be sorry you came after me."

Partner? What in the world was he talking about? I didn't have a partner on this boat, in the business sense or any other.

I didn't really spend a lot of time pondering that, though, because I was too busy panicking and fighting, trying to get away from him. I twisted and writhed, stomped on his feet, kicked back at his shins, tried to elbow him in the stomach. None of it did a bit of good. I couldn't get away, couldn't yell, couldn't even bite Rafferty's hand, because he was holding me too tightly. I lifted a leg and tried to kick Gallister's door, but Rafferty pulled me away so that the kick fell short.

My heart pounded so wildly in my chest it felt like it was about to burst right through my skin. I knew now that the initial dislike and distrust I'd felt toward Rafferty were justified. So was the outright suspicion that he was a killer. I felt his murderous intent in his big, strong hands as he backed onto the deck and dragged me with him.

He paused when he was just outside the door. I felt his chin brush the back of my hair as he quickly turned his head from one side to the other and then back. Checking to see if the coast was clear, I thought. He didn't want anybody to see him dragging me to wherever he planned to take me.

Wherever he planned to get rid of me.

If I had cooperated and gone with him without raising a fuss, I'm sure he would have taken me to some isolated spot below decks and then broken my neck, too. As it was, I didn't think he would try to negotiate several flights of stairs and a couple of decks with a struggling woman. So I wasn't all that surprised when he hauled me toward the stairs leading up to the pilothouse. Shocked in one way, maybe, but not really surprised. He craned his neck to look over the railing along the edge of the deck, checking below to see if anyone was watching, then started dragging me up the stairs.

I was scared, mad, and determined, all at the same time, but even though I kept fighting I was no match for Rafferty's strength and brutality. I winced in pain as his hands tightened even more. I got both feet planted against one of the steps above him and shoved with them as hard as I could, hoping that would force him to topple over backward, but he didn't budge. I knew I might be hurt if we both fell down the stairs, but that seemed less dangerous than letting him take me wherever he wanted.

There was no "wherever" about it, I realized. There could be only one destination.

The pilothouse.

We reached the top of the stairs. Rafferty obviously didn't want to let go of me with either hand, so he kicked the door, just like I'd tried to kick Gallister's door. This one opened a second later, and Captain L. B. Williams looked out with a puzzled expression on his face that turned into one of pure shock when he recognized me and Rafferty.

"What the hell—" he began.

"Get out of the way," Rafferty growled.

Williams stepped back, and Rafferty all but threw me into the pilothouse. He came in fast right behind me, heeling the door closed as he did so, and put both hands on my shoulders to force me down into a chair.

"What are you doing?" Williams demanded.

"Cleaning up a mess," Rafferty snapped.

Then he did something I didn't really expect, even though I knew how much danger I was in.

He drew back a fist and punched me in the face.

I went out like the proverbial light.

Funny thing about being knocked out. It's not at all like being asleep. You don't dream. There's no sense of time passing. It's just nothing. It's not even blackness, because that implies the possibility of something other than blackness.

The moments when you're regaining consciousness are the only ones that even remotely resemble sleep. You begin to be aware of things, but only vaguely, like when you start to come out of a deep, almost drugged slumber. Gradually you figure out that you're lying down and you can't see anything because your eyes are closed. You hear distorted noises that make no sense. You feel the surface underneath you—a nice, soft bed if you're lucky.

The hard wooden floor of a riverboat pilothouse if you're not.

The harsh noises that filtered into my ears slowly became voices. The part of my brain that was beginning to function again recognized them after a while. They belonged to Logan Rafferty and Captain Williams. And the captain, bless his heart, was saying, ". . . won't allow you to kill her."

"You don't have any choice in the matter," Rafferty told him. "She's a danger to us."

"And having yet another dead body show up won't endanger us?" Williams asked.

It was a logical question, I thought. I knew they were talking about me, but at that point I wasn't quite able to grasp that my continued survival depended on what they were saying. My brain hadn't come that far back yet.

"Look, I overheard Gallister talking to his lawyers. He said something about a PI. It's got to be this Dickinson broad. She's been poking around and asking questions practically ever since she came on board. Then I caught her coming out of Gallister's suite. She's got to be working for him."

"Did it ever occur to you that she's really a travel agent and was just concerned because one of her clients had been killed?"

"Webster?" Rafferty snorted. "I'll bet he was a PI, too. They were probably working together."

He was way off on that, I thought. Or was he? Since "Ben Webster" was a phony identity, maybe the dead man, whatever his name really was, had been working undercover, too, just like Mark. And, for that matter, Vince Mallory.

One thing I've learned running tours is that if you take any group of people, anywhere, among them will be plenty of secrets, most of which the folks who hold them don't want revealed. Most of those secrets aren't that important to the world at large. Chances are, anybody who found out about them wouldn't really care. Certainly some secrets are more shameful than others. Occasionally somebody might actually get into trouble with the law if the things that person was hiding were brought out into the open. Mostly, though, the secrets that people hide are harmless.

Boy, that wasn't true on this cruise. False identities, private detectives working undercover, mistresses, murders, crooked gambling . . . Obviously, what went on aboard the *Southern Belle* wasn't nearly as genteel as the boat's name might lead you to expect.

But Rafferty was sure wrong about one thing: I wasn't a private eye. I didn't think Webster had been, either, but I didn't know for sure about that.

"Did you find anything on her computer?" Williams asked.

"Just travel agency stuff. It's a good cover. I'll bet there are some hidden files on there somewhere, though. I'll keep looking."

So Rafferty was the one who had taken my computer! The ransacking of my cabin hadn't been a simple burglary after all. He'd been looking for proof that I was a private detective, possibly working with Ben Webster.

I might have laughed if I hadn't wanted them to think I was still unconscious. Rafferty and Williams were worried that a private eye might be on the boat looking into their activities. They had no idea that Mark Lansing really was a PI, but the case that had brought him here had nothing to do with the rigged gambling going on in the casino. Rafferty had suspected me before Gallister ever came aboard and said something that Rafferty had overheard and taken as confirmation of his suspicions. In truth, Gallister had been talking about Mark, but Rafferty had no way of knowing that. He had just jumped to the conclusion that he'd been right about me all along.

If my head hadn't hurt already from being punched, it probably would have ached from trying to follow all the crazy thoughts whirling around in my head. Too many murders, too many motives . . .

"You always jump the gun," Williams complained with a note of bitter resentment in his voice. "If you hadn't panicked when that Kramer girl figured out what Garvey was doing—"

"If I hadn't taken care of her, she would have told Gallister. Who do you think he would have believed? Us or her?"

"Her, I suppose," Williams said. "He was sleeping with her, after all." He sighed. "Still, you didn't have to kill her. You didn't have to kill that young man yesterday."

"I didn't," Rafferty snapped. "I didn't have anything to do with what happened to Webster."

"What?" I heard the surprise in Williams's voice. "I just assumed—"

"Well, you were wrong."

I bit back a groan. Not only did I hurt, but the revelations were coming fast and furious now. Rafferty had just admitted killing Hannah Kramer. Not to protect his boss, Gallister, though. From the sound of it, Gallister hadn't known anything about Hannah's death. He might be guilty of a lot of things, but evidently murder wasn't one of them.

At the same time, Rafferty denied killing Ben Webster, and as far as I could see, he wouldn't have any reason to lie about that to his own partner in crime, which Williams obviously was. If that was true, who had killed Webster?

I lay there trying to keep my breathing even so they'd think I was still out cold, and as I did I thought back over everything that had happened since I came on board the *Southern Belle*. I would have said that as much as I'd mulled over all the facts of both cases during the past day and a half, I must have considered every conceivable possibility, every theory no matter how far-fetched. . . .

But then I realized there was one theory that had never crossed my mind. One question with an obvious answer that I had overlooked. One answer that tied everything together while, unfortunately, raising even more questions.

Those new questions would never be answered unless I could get out of here somehow. A part of me still wanted to panic, to start crying and begging for mercy, but I knew Rafferty didn't have any mercy to give. He had proven that with the callous way he had gotten rid of Hannah Kramer once she realized that the roulette wheel in the casino was crooked. Had she tried to cut herself in on the action? That didn't seem likely to me, but I didn't know. Maybe she had thought Garvey was working the scheme on his own and had reported him to Rafferty, never realizing until it was too late that Garvey was working for Rafferty. At this late date, that didn't really matter. All that was important was that Rafferty was a killer—and he planned on getting rid of me next.

So, no, I couldn't beg for mercy. I had to get away somehow, or get help to come to me.

All those thoughts had gone through my head in a matter of seconds. Williams said, "If you didn't kill Webster, who did?"

"I don't know and I don't care, except that it got that bitch cop nosing around. Still, she's got no idea what's really been going on, and as long as the casino's closed down, she won't find out."

Williams snapped, "The casino can stay closed down, as far as I'm concerned. It's bad enough that this beautiful old boat was turned into Gallister's own private, floating brothel."

Yeah, he was old-fashioned, all right. Old-fashioned enough to let his resentment over Gallister using the riverboat for philandering justify his own involvement in Rafferty's crooked gambling operation. I had wanted to like and respect Captain Williams, but not anymore. He couldn't justify Hannah Kramer's murder.

Rafferty gave a harsh laugh. "You weren't too proud to take your cut from the money we made," he said, echoing the sentiment that had just gone through my head. I can't tell you how much it bothered me that Logan Rafferty and I would think alike about *anything*. "Look, keep your head in the sand if you want to," he went on. "I don't care. Just let me take care of things."

"What are you . . . what are you going to do with her?"

"I haven't decided yet, but I'll make it look like an accident, you can count on that."

"Like you did with Hannah Kramer?"

"That would have looked like an accident, damn it, if that nosy passenger hadn't spotted her in the water too soon. That wasn't my fault."

"No," Williams said. "Nothing is ever your fault, is it?"

Maybe they would argue so much that a fight would break out between them, I thought desperately, even though I knew it was unlikely that Williams would want to take on a bruiser like Rafferty. But if that happened, maybe I could use the distraction to jump up and try to get away. If I could just get out of the pilothouse, I planned to start yelling my lungs out.

They didn't start fighting, though. Instead, Williams went on, "Ms. Dickinson has been spending quite a bit of time with Lansing, that actor who plays Mark Twain in the salon. If she disappears, he's liable to start looking for her."

"I'm not worried about some damn actor," Rafferty said with contempt in his voice. "If he gives us any trouble, he can disappear, too."

"Yes, just kill everyone. That's an excellent solution to our problems."

Rafferty laughed again. "What's that old saying? They can only hang me once."

Even though I like to think I'm not a violent person at heart, the mental image of Rafferty at the end of a rope was pretty appealing right then. But even stronger was the worry and fear I felt for Mark. Because Williams was right: Mark would try to find out what had happened to me.

And even though Rafferty was underestimating him, I wasn't convinced that Mark was really a match for him.

Even as upset as I was, I heard the faint noise that came from somewhere nearby. I opened one eye the narrowest crack and found that my head was turned toward the door into the pilot-house. I saw the knob turning ever so slowly, as if somebody was trying to open it without Rafferty and Williams hearing.

Mark! That thought leaped into my mind. He had figured out somehow that I was being held prisoner up here, and he had come to rescue me. Normally I would think that I could take care of myself, thank you very much, and wasn't the sort of woman who needed rescuing—but under the circumstances I'd take any sort of knight right about now, even one in tinfoil armor.

But then Rafferty said, "What the hell was that?" and started to turn toward the door.

Without thinking too much about what I was doing, I groaned and pushed myself onto my hands and knees, like a person who has suddenly regained consciousness. I crawled toward the other side of the pilothouse, trying to draw their attention away from the door.

It worked. Rafferty snapped, "Damn it, she's awake! Grab her!"

"You grab her!" Williams said.

Neither of them grabbed me, although Rafferty took a long step toward me. Still groaning to cover up any sounds the door made as it opened, I reached a chart table against the wall and took hold of it. I used it to steady myself as I climbed shakily to my feet. The shakiness wasn't an act. I was dizzy from being knocked out. The room spun crazily around me.

But I could see well enough to recognize not Mark, but rather Vince Mallory, as he stepped into the pilothouse, leveled a gun at Williams and Rafferty, and said, "Don't move, either of you."

CHAPTER 25

Relief didn't exactly flood through me, but just then I was glad to see Vince anyway.

The feeling didn't last long, because Rafferty grabbed my arm, jerked me in front of him like a human shield, and rushed at Vince, who couldn't fire without hitting me. We crashed together. The impact knocked Vince backward, and he almost toppled backward down the stairs. He flung out his free hand and grabbed the doorjamb just in time to keep from falling.

I twisted out of the way, but unfortunately, that gave Rafferty the room he needed to throw a roundhouse punch. His fist slammed into Vince's jaw. Somehow, Vince managed to hang on to the doorjamb. He lifted his leg and drove a kick into Rafferty's belly.

Earlier, I hadn't been able to do any good hitting Rafferty's stomach, which seemed as hard as a rock. Vince was stronger and trained for combat, though. His kick made Rafferty turn pale and stagger back a couple of steps. Vince leaped forward and swung the gun in his hand. It thudded hard against Rafferty's skull. Rafferty's eyes rolled up in his head as his knees unhinged. He crumpled to the pilothouse floor.

I made a leap for the door, but Vince was too fast for me. He caught the collar of my blouse and swung me back inside. I crashed against the chart table. Pain shot through my hip where I ran into the table. I slapped my hands against the table to keep from falling.

Vince leveled the gun at a stunned Captain Williams and said, "Call the engine room. Tell them to start getting up steam."

Williams gawked at him for a second, then said, "We . . . we can't go anywhere. The police—"

"Don't worry about them," Vince interrupted. "Just do what I told you."

"But the mooring lines—"

"I've already cast off." A faint smile appeared on Vince's face. "That's what I was doing, or I would have been up here sooner after I saw Rafferty manhandling Ms. Dickinson up the stairs." Vince paused, then gave Rafferty a vicious kick to the ribs. I heard at least one of them crack under the impact. Rafferty groaned from the pain and stirred slightly but didn't regain consciousness.

"Young man—" Williams said.

Vince took a step toward him, thrusting the gun out so that the barrel stabbed almost between the captain's eyes. "Do it!" he ordered. "Get the engines started!"

Williams didn't have any color in his face anymore. He jerked his head in a nod and reached for the old-fashioned speaking tube that connected the pilothouse to the engine room. "We'll be leaving shortly," he said. "Prepare the engines. Get up steam."

As a matter of fact, I could already feel the boat moving a little more than usual, confirming that Vince had cast off the thick mooring ropes that held the *Southern Belle* to the dock. The Mississippi's inexorable current was tugging at it, but here along the shore it wasn't strong enough to sweep the boat out into the river. The engines would have to do that.

Vince glanced at me and said, "I hope I didn't hurt you, Ms. Dickinson. I couldn't have you running around the boat telling everybody what's going on, though. There's not much time left."

"Time for what?" I asked. I had the glimmering of an idea, but that was all.

"Until the anniversary," he said, and that was enough to make the remaining pieces of the puzzle slide together in my head and form a picture.

"You knew Hannah in St. Louis, didn't you?" I said. "You were dating her before she got involved with Gallister."

"We were more than dating," he snapped. "We were going to be married. Then she met that bastard Gallister, and his smarmy charm and all his money swept her away. If it hadn't been for him, we'd be a family by now, Hannah and the baby and me."

"But Gallister got her the job on this riverboat, and then she forgot all about you, didn't she?" I wanted to keep him talking, both to understand fully what was going on here and to delay him from proceeding with whatever his plans were.

"That's right," he admitted. "Gallister and this boat ruined everything." He smiled again. "So I'm glad that Gallister is aboard. That was a stroke of luck. It saves me from having to settle with him later. I can take care of everything at once."

"What about Hannah's parents?" I asked. "They're on board, too, you know. You can't have anything against them."

His expression hardened. "They're to blame, too. Her father told her to move out if she wanted to. If she hadn't, she never would have wound up on this boat, one year ago tonight."

"But if she hadn't moved out, you never would have met her in St. Louis," I pointed out. "You should be thankful for that."

He gave a little shake of his head, not like he was disagreeing with me but rather as if he was trying to make sense of everything. Then he scowled and said, "It doesn't make any difference. They were part of it. They have to pay like everybody else."

The hatred he had been nursing ever since Hannah's death was too strong for him to let go of it, no matter what I said. He'd been in love, and he'd lost her, and everyone else was to blame, not him. I suddenly found myself wondering just how real the so-called love affair between him and Hannah really had been. Had they actually talked about marriage, or was that all in Vince Mallory's head? Was he really the father of Hannah's baby?

I didn't know, but all that could be sorted out later—if there *was* a later. I had a bad feeling about Vince's plans.

A quiver went through the floor under my feet. It came from the engines being fired up, I figured. A second later the speaking tube squawked, confirming that. Vince gestured toward it with the gun and told Williams, "Ask them how long until they have full power."

Williams did as he was told, and whoever was down in the engine room reported that they'd have full steam in ten or fifteen minutes. I realized there was a clock mounted on the wall of the pilothouse. It was just past eight o'clock.

Mark's performance as Mark Twain would be getting under way in the salon.

Vince nodded. "That's good," he told the captain. "Eight thirty-seven is the time."

"Wh-what time?" Williams asked.

"The time of vengeance," Vince said.

"The time Hannah died," I said.

Vince glanced at me again. "One year ago, to the minute. Everyone for miles around will know that she's been avenged."

Oh, Lordy, Lordy, I thought. That sounded really bad. It takes a mighty big noise for folks to be able to hear it for miles around.

Like an explosion so powerful that it would blow an entire riverboat into little-bitty pieces of kindling.

"You weren't an MP at all, were you?" I guessed. "You were in demolitions. You and your buddy Ben, or whatever his name really was."

His voice was sharp as he asked, "What did he tell you?"

"Don't worry, he didn't betray you. He didn't tell me anything about what you were planning to do."

"It was only a matter of time," Vince said bitterly. "He was getting cold feet. He said that all the people on board didn't deserve to die, that they hadn't had anything to do with what had happened to Hannah. He didn't understand that this was the only way I could be sure of punishing the ones who were really to blame."

"He did it!" Williams cried in a voice ragged with panic. He pointed at the unconscious man on the floor. "Rafferty killed that girl! I had nothing to do with it!"

Vince looked down at Rafferty, and for a second I thought he was going to empty the gun into him. But then Vince shook his head and said, "It's too late to stop things now. Everybody has to pay. Gallister, Hannah's folks, this boat itself. This damn riverboat . . ."

"And when Ben didn't want to go along with that, you killed him," I said. "That was your cabin he went to yesterday, but it wasn't an accident or a ruse to get away from me. He wanted to talk to you, to tell you that he was backing out of the deal you'd made with him."

That was what I had realized earlier. I had never considered the possibility that there might be a connection between Webster and Vince. It had seemed to be pure chance that I had made Vince's acquaintance, and I had accepted it as that. Circumstances and his natural likeability— or his carefully calculated *pose* of natural likeability—had blinded me to what was really going on.

"Todd and I swore over there that we'd back each other up once we got home, just like we did in Iraq," Vince said, his voice trembling with anger. "It was all lies. When it came time to seek vengeance for Hannah, he went along at first, but then he tried to double-cross me. He came to my cabin and said that there had been some trouble, said that the head of security for the boat would be keeping an eye on him and we ought to just call off the plan. When I told him we couldn't do that, he panicked. I knew I couldn't trust him."

"So you killed him," I said. "Broke his neck."

"I convinced him to go below decks with me," Vince said with a shrug. "I told him I wanted his opinion on where I'd decided to plant the bomb—"

"Bomb!" Captain Williams said. I was surprised he hadn't tumbled to what was going on before now.

Vince ignored him and went on, "Of course, that's not really where I planted it. There's a better place. But I knew the security cameras don't cover that little hall by the engine room, and I was able to take him down there by a route that doesn't show up much on the cameras. Anywhere there was a chance the cameras might catch us, I made sure our faces were averted."

"You must have studied the layout of this boat before you ever came aboard," I said.

"Actually, I did, but I've also been aboard eight times in the past year, taking the cruise under various names and using disguises. Preparation is the key to a successful mission. The army taught me that, too."

"Along with how to blow up stuff real good," I muttered.

"Yeah," Vince said with a laugh. "That, too."

The engine room called then on the speaking tube, reporting that full steam was up. Vince nodded to Captain Williams. "Take us out into the river," he ordered. "Cruise south."

"Detective Travis must have left officers on the dock," Williams said. "They'll stop us."

"No, they won't," Vince replied with a shake of his head. "I knocked both of them out before I cast off. I showed them my badge, and I was close enough to take them out before they knew what was going on."

"Badge?" Williams croaked.

"You're not really an investigator for the attorney general, are you?" I asked. "That was another lie."

"It comes in handy sometimes," he said with a shrug. "Like when you're trying to get the blueprints of a riverboat to study."

"Why'd you follow Mark and me into the casino earlier today?"

"I saw the two of you sneaking around and wanted to know what you were up to. I eavesdropped on you long enough to figure out that the roulette wheel is rigged before I let you know I was there. That was interesting. I thought maybe it had something to do with what happened to Hannah."

"It had everything to do with her murder," I said. "She found out about the rigged games—"

"And Rafferty killed her," Williams said again. "I tell you, I had nothing to do with it, and no one else on this boat is to blame."

"Gallister is," Vince said. "Her parents are. You are, too. Anyway, it doesn't matter." He gestured with the gun. "Take us out into the river," he said in a flat voice.

Williams swallowed hard and gave the order through the speaking tube, just like in the old days. "Back one-quarter."

Another shiver went through the deck. I felt the slow, ponderous power of the engines as the paddlewheels began to revolve and push the boat away from the dock. The engine room crew wouldn't know what was going on, but they probably figured that we'd been cleared to leave Hannibal. They had their orders; that was all that would matter to them.

Williams spun the wheel as the *Southern Belle* left the dock behind and moved out into the flow of the river. He gave the order to stop engines. From the window of the pilothouse I saw water sluicing from the paddlewheels as they slowed to a halt. Then Williams ordered, "Ahead three-quarters." The wheels began to turn the other way, biting into the water, propelling us southward in conjunction with the current. Below, people began to come out on deck, no doubt wondering what was going on and why we were cruising downriver in the dark like this.

"Are you really a reader of Mark Twain, Vince?" I asked. I knew that Vince Mallory probably wasn't his real name; no doubt it was another of his phony identities. But I didn't know what else to call him.

"I love Twain's work," he said. "Always have. How can you not, growing up in this part of the country?"

"Then you know from readin' *Life on the Mississippi* that it's dangerous for a boat to be out on the river at night. We're liable to hit a hidden snag."

He glanced at the clock on the wall, which now read eight-twenty. "In seventeen more minutes, it won't matter," he said.

"No," Williams said suddenly. "No, I won't let you do it."

"It's too late now. Hannah will be avenged."

The lights of Hannibal were falling behind us. From the corner of my eye I saw flashing red and blue lights approaching the waterfront. Maybe one of the cops Vince had knocked out had come to and called for help. Maybe they had figured out some other way that something was going on. It didn't matter. They were too late to stop the *Southern Belle* from heading downstream.

"Get back," Vince said, lifting the gun as Williams took a step toward him.

"This is my boat," the captain declared. "I don't care who owns it. It's *my* boat, and I won't see it harmed."

"Get back, blast it!"

Williams ignored the warning. He leaped at Vince and reached for the gun.

The shot was deafeningly loud in the relatively close confines of the pilothouse. I didn't see smoke or flame gush from the barrel. There was just the roar of the shot, and then Williams was falling back against the wheel with blood welling from the hole in his chest and staining his uniform jacket. He flung out one hand and grabbed a spoke in an attempt to catch himself, and that caused the wheel to spin as Williams fell to the floor.

The riverboat began to turn.

At the same time I realized that Rafferty had pulled the same trick as I had earlier. He had been playing possum, pretending to be unconscious as he listened to what the rest of us were saying. Now he twisted around and kicked out at Vince's legs, catching him on the side of a knee. Vince cried out in pain and fell. Rafferty went after him, trying to get his hands around Vince's neck.

Vince slashed at him with the gun, raking it across Rafferty's face. Crimson spurted from a cut on Rafferty's forehead opened up by the gun's sight. Vince hit him again, breaking his nose this time. Rafferty groaned and sagged back. Vince crashed the gun down in his face twice more. I thought I heard bone splintering. Vince's face twisted in lines of insane hatred.

I didn't see any more. I lunged for the doorway, my injured hip slowing me down a little.

But I made it out the door despite that and

started down the stairs toward the third deck. I had taken only a couple of steps when a familiar voice called, "Delilah!"

I looked down and saw Mark Twain at the bottom of the stairs, white suit, bushy mustache and all. But I thought I either had lost my mind or was seeing things, because there were four Mark Twains in all, scattered along the deck near the bottom of the stairs, peering up at me. I stopped, blinked, shook my head.

Then Vince flung the door to the pilothouse open behind me, stepped out, and started shooting. I saw one of the Mark Twains go down.

"Mark!" I cried, but I wasn't talking about the writer. I had recognized Mark Lansing's voice when he called my name, and for all I knew, he was the Twain who was hit.

Furious, I turned and threw myself at Vince's legs, driving my body into them as hard as I could. The collision upended him and made him fall over me with a startled cry. He hit the stairs and continued bouncing down them toward the third deck. I couldn't tell if he still had the gun or if the fall had caused him to drop it.

The closest Mark Twain charged up the stairs and landed on Vince before Vince hit the bottom. He crashed a fist into Vince's face—once, twice, three times—as hard and fast as he could, then leaped over Vince's senseless form and hurried on up the stairs to me. I felt his hands on my arms. They pulled me up, and Mark Lansing said, "Delilah! Delilah, are you okay?"

So he wasn't the Twain who'd been shot. I

took a second to be grateful for that, then gasped, "What time is it?"

"What?" Mark asked, clearly startled that I'd be wondering about such a thing right now.

"What time is it?" I repeated.

Mark let go of me with one hand and used it to pull an old-fashioned turnip pocket watch out of the watch pocket of his vest. "This is a prop, but it keeps good time," he said. "I've got eight thirty. Why?"

"Because in seven minutes," I told him, "a bomb is gonna blow this riverboat to kingdom come."

CHAPTER 26

There's nothing like the word *bomb* to make folks go nuts. Usually with good cause, of course. The other Mark Twains heard it, including the wounded one, who was on his feet again and obviously not hurt too bad, and they took off, yelling at the top of their lungs.

Mark's hands tightened on my shoulders. "A bomb?" he repeated. "Are you sure?"

I nodded. "It's too long a story to go into right now, but I'm sure." Something Vince had said earlier popped up in my mind. "And I think I know where it is. You've seen the police reports. Where was Hannah killed?"

Mark frowned. "As far as the cops could determine, she was struck on the head and then thrown into the paddlewheel from the third deck."

I believed it. Rafferty was big enough and strong enough to throw an unconscious young woman that far, so that she'd clear the lower decks and fall into the paddlewheel.

That jibed with what I'd thought. I said, "Come on," and pushed past Mark to start down the steps.

He followed close behind me, steadying me with a hand on my arm. "Delilah, we've got to get off this boat."

"There's no time," I told him. "We couldn't swim far enough away to be safe. And there's no way everybody could get off in time." We stepped over Vince, who was still sprawled near the bottom of the stairs, out cold. I glanced up-river toward Hannibal and saw flashing lights coming toward us. A police boat, I figured. But it wouldn't get there in time, either.

"What are you going to do?" Mark asked. "Disarm the damn bomb?"

He had me there. I didn't know anything about disarming bombs.

"I don't reckon you know how to do that?" I asked him.

He shook his head.

"Well, come on," I said. "Maybe we can get the blasted thing off the boat."

I went at a run toward the observation deck. Vince had been sitting there when I'd found him earlier in the day, and he'd had a backpack with him, I recalled. And this was the place where Hannah had been killed. What more appropriate spot than that to plant his instrument of vengeance for her?

I started jerking open the doors of the storage areas underneath the benches. Mark got the idea and started helping. After only a cou-

ple of seconds, he recoiled like he'd found a
snake and said, "Son of a—! Delilah, over here."

I hurried to his side and bent down to look.
The light wasn't good, but there was enough for
me to see the simple-looking box, about a foot
square, with some wires and a cheap, battery-
powered digital clock attached to it. The read-
out on the clock said *7:35*.

Two minutes left.

I reached for the box. Mark grabbed my
wrist, stopping me. "What if it's rigged to go off
instantly if anybody disturbs it?"

"It's not," I said, trying to put some conviction in my voice. "Vince didn't think anybody
would find it. It's just a simple device, the kind
the insurgents in Iraq used. Vince probably saw
a lot of 'em over there."

"You can't know that," Mark said.

The last number in the display switched from
5 to *6*.

"It's gonna blow up in another minute anyway," I said.

Mark said, "Yeah," and reached past me. Before I could stop him, he picked up the bomb.

It didn't go off. He turned and ran for the
rail and when he got there he heaved that box
as hard as he could. I lost sight of it in the dark,
but I heard the splash as it hit the water.

"Noooo!" Vince screamed behind us.

We turned and saw him standing there looking horrified and grief stricken, and then somebody kicked his knee from behind and brought
him down. Detective Charlotte Travis landed on

top of him, planting a knee in the small of his back to pin him to the deck as she grabbed his arms and brought them behind him. He didn't fight her as she slipped plastic restraints around his wrists. He had failed to avenge his lost love, and nothing else mattered to him.

Travis looked up at Mark and me and said, "Does somebody want to tell me what in the world—"

That was when the bomb went off.

I had hoped that being dumped in the Mississippi would deactivate it, or whatever you call it, but clearly, that wasn't the case. The *Southern Belle* literally jumped as the force of the explosion shot through the river. Water flew a hundred feet or more in the air and came back down like a sudden thunderstorm. The explosion had sounded like thunder, muffled as it was by the river. The current increased suddenly like a tsunami, and for a second it felt like we were flying.

But the vast waters of the Mississippi also acted to spread out the power of the blast, and as the water flung high into the air pattered back down, the effects began to subside. We had all been jolted off our feet by the initial concussion, but now we were able to sit up.

"Was that a *bomb*?" Travis asked.

That seemed like a pretty dumb question to me. It must have to her, too, once she thought about it, because she glared at me and said, "I hope you can explain all of this, Ms. Dickinson."

"Why me?" I asked.

"Well, it's either you or Mark Twain," she said as she got to her feet, nodding toward Mark.

" 'Every man is a moon and has a dark side,' " Mark quoted.

Travis frowned. "What?"

I pointed to Vince Mallory. "He showed his dark side. We'll tell you all about it, but first you'd better go on up to the pilothouse. I reckon you'll find another killer up there."

Rafferty was still in the pilothouse, all right. He wasn't going anywhere, not with the fractured skull Vince had given him. He died in a St. Louis hospital two days later without regaining consciousness.

Captain L. B. Williams was already dead when the police reached the pilothouse. Vince's bullet had nicked his heart, and he'd bled to death.

Clyde Garvey spilled everything about the crooked gambling in the casino, though, and was quick to implicate Rafferty in Hannah Kramer's murder. He and Williams had both known what Rafferty had done to cover up their scheme.

I was the only one who could testify as to what Vince had said about killing Ben Webster, but he never denied it in court. The trial six months later resulted in him being convicted on one count of murder, two counts of voluntary manslaughter, and multiple counts of attempted murder since he'd tried to blow up the *Southern Belle* with everybody on it. His attorney tried to argue the insanity defense, using testimony from army psychiatrists who said that Vince had been dishonorably discharged for the mental problems he had exhibited when he was in the service, but the jury found him guilty anyway. He had enough life sentences stacked consecutively that he'd never see the outside of a prison again. Of course, he would probably spend that time in a prison mental ward, since he went catatonic following his conviction and showed no signs of coming out of it.

I didn't think it really mattered much, one way or the other. Vincent Meadows—his real name—was in a prison of his own making and would never get out of it.

Ben Webster's real name, by the way, was Todd Shepherd. From what I learned later, they had indeed been best friends while serving in Iraq. Shepherd had tried to rein in Meadows's violent, obsessive tendencies, according to other soldiers who knew them. Unfortunately, he had failed.

As far as Detective Travis was ever able to find out, Vince had dated Hannah Kramer exactly twice. From those two dates, he had spun out the whole fantasy about them having a future together. Evidently he had lived in a world of his own, and had for quite a while. That was one reason he was able to adopt different identities so easily and convincingly. To Vince, nothing was real except his own fantasies.

Learning all that came later, though. That night, once the riverboat was docked at Hannibal again and everything had settled down, what

I wanted to know was where those extra Mark Twains had come from.

"They perform as Twain in dinner theaters here in town," Mark explained with a smile as we sat on the observation deck with Louise and Eddie Kramer. He had taken off the wig and mustache and make-up but still wore the white suit. "They're all friends, so they decided to come over here between their shows and take in my performance. Checking out the competition, as it were. The cops let them come on board, since Detective Travis just said to keep the passengers and crew from getting off."

Louise said, "I heard that one of them was wounded. Not badly, I hope?"

Mark shook his head. "Grazed his arm, that's all. I'm sure it hurt like blazes, but it's not a serious injury."

"How'd you all show up on the third deck like that, at just the right time?" I asked.

"Everybody knew something was wrong when the boat left the dock like that, without any announcement or anything," Mark explained. "I just had a hunch you were mixed up in it somehow, Delilah, and went looking for you. The other guys came with me. I was going to start by asking Captain Williams if he'd seen you, as well as trying to find out why we were headed downriver." He smiled. "Luck was on our side, I guess."

Eddie said, "I don't think we can ever thank you enough for finding out what happened to our little girl, Mark."

Again, Mark shook his head. He pointed at

me. "Delilah did that. She kept poking around until Rafferty finally made a move against her, just like he did with Hannah. Thank God it didn't end up the same."

"I wish it hadn't ended like that with Hannah," I said.

Eddie sighed. "We can't change the past. Lord knows, I sometimes wish we could."

Louise slid both of her arms around his right arm as she sat beside him. "But we'll hold the good memories in our hearts forever," she said. "Nobody can take those away from us."

We sat there in silence for a while longer, and then Eddie and Louise went back to their cabin, leaving Mark and me alone on one of the benches. The police had already gone over the observation deck, since this was where Vince had hidden the bomb, but there really wasn't anything to find. They had taken down the crime scene tape.

"It seems strange that right where we're sittin', there was a bomb that nearly blew us all sky-high," I said.

" 'Truth is stranger than fiction, but it is because fiction is obliged to stick to possibilities; truth isn't.' "

"Mark Twain?"

"Yep. It's from *Pudd'nhead Wilson.* Most of his really famous sayings are. I like this one, too: 'Let us endeavor so to live that when we die, even the undertaker will be sorry.' "

"Well, the undertaker's gonna have to wait a while for me," I said. "I've got to get this tour group back to St. Louis and then head home to Atlanta."

"Think you might ever want to cruise the Mississippi again?"

"You don't plan to stay on as Mark Twain, do you?"

He shook his head. "No. I sort of enjoyed it, but I'm a detective, not an actor. I thought I might take this cruise again as a passenger, though, one of these days. You think I could book it through your agency?"

"Nothing stoppin' you," I told him. I didn't stop him when he slipped an arm around my shoulders, either.

The mighty Mississippi kept rolling, and I figured that for a while, I would just roll right along with it.

Hannibal, Missouri

Sometimes known as America's hometown, Hannibal is thoroughly modern while retaining its historic charm. Most of the attractions in the area, appropriately enough, center around Mark Twain and his life and work.

The Mark Twain Boyhood Home & Museum complex includes eight buildings in Hannibal, six of historical significance and two serving as interactive museums. Featured in the museum collections are fifteen original paintings by another master of Americana, Norman Rockwell. Self-guided tours of the Mark Twain Boyhood Home & Museum properties are available and give tourists and literary buffs a chance to explore the Hannibal of Samuel Clemens's childhood and experience the beloved stories he created as Mark Twain through the power of his imagination. To discover how a young boy growing up in the small village of Hannibal became one of the world's most beloved authors, start by visiting www.marktwainmuseum.org.

Numerous riverboats stop at Hannibal on excursion cruises up and down the Mississippi River, and the Mark Twain Riverboat, with its home port in Hannibal, offers one-hour sightseeing tours of the river, two-hour dinner cruises, and special jazz cruises. More information is available at http://marktwainriverboat.com.

The caves that served as the inspiration for scenes in *The Adventures of Tom Sawyer* are located near Hannibal. Now known as Mark Twain Cave and Campground, this natural attraction was first opened to the public in 1886 and is a registered natural landmark. The cave is cool and comfortable and the tours are easy to walk, but because of the narrowness of the passages it is not wheelchair accessible. A visitor's center, gift shop, fudge shop, and rock shop are also located at the cave complex. In Cave Hollow Center, noted actor and Mark Twain impersonator Jim Waddell performs in "The Life and Times of Mark Twain." Check out http://marktwaincave.com and www.MarkTwainLives.com for more information.

Dinner theaters in Hannibal include the Planters Barn Theater, featuring performances of "Mark Twain Himself" (http://marktwainhimself.com) and the Spratt Family Theater (http://sprattfamilyjubilee.com). All the attractions in Hannibal can be visited by hopping on one of the sightseeing tours conducted by the Hannibal Trolley Company, the Twainland Express, or the Mark Twain Clopper (a horse-drawn trolley).

The Web site of the Hannibal Convention & Visitors Bureau is located at http://visithannibal.com. Visitors are advised to check with the bureau for the current status of Hannibal's various attractions when planning a trip to the area.